BROTHERS OF THE ZODIAC

WATER

MAXWELL THOMAS

Cover design © 2017 by Niki Lenhart
nikilen-designs.com

Published by Zarra Knightley Publishing
zarraknightleypublishing.com

ISBN 978-1-946907-10-3 (Trade Paperback)

10 9 8 7 6 5 4 3 2 1

FIRST EDITION

To Jon, Joel, and Chris,
who instructed me in ERP.

PROLOGUE

SPRING, CIRCA 3500 BC
UR, MESOPOTAMIA

PROLOGUE

GIRTAB PATTED HIMSELF DOWN. The knives were hidden in his skirt, among the folds of fur that he had sewn in for just that purpose. It was chilly tonight, so he could get away with the ram's-skin skirt.

He was going to meet the Brothers tonight. Although the way would be brightly lit, the way back would be dark, and he didn't want to get caught unawares. He would walk with Saj most of the way back. But here, toward the north half of the wharf where he lived, no one really had homes, except thieves and the slaves he hadn't sold.

Girtab locked the door and started away from his home. He headed west, to the northern part of the city, to the White Temple. There, the Brothers would meet, and reiterate their quest to the Lady.

Girtab had called this meeting because of what he had seen two days ago. Gud, the Bull, had come to his slave market, even though he was provided slaves — and more — with his position in the palace.

Girtab grinned. How ironic that the man who had succeeded in rushing the bulls during a celebration of Gilgamesh's victory over the Bull of Heaven would be the man to kill him.

The Lady Ishtar blessed him, as she had blessed all the Brothers, with abilities beyond those of even Gilgamesh and Enkidu. With this blessing, however, came this quest: they must kill Gilgamesh. Gilgamesh had vanquished the Bull of Heaven, who had been sent by Ishtar's sister to punish Gilgamesh for repudiating Ishtar. Now she had men to kill Gilgamesh.

Except, they needed to be reminded every once in a while.

It had been three years, and each of the Brothers had partially gone their separate ways in the city of Ur. Three years while they bided their time. Girtab knew it was time.

Girtab turned the corner and literally bumped into an archer in full regalia.

"Saj!"

"Girtab!"

They clasped their forearms and looked into each other's black eyes. Both men were dark skinned and bald. Saj carried a bow and a quiver, and wore a necklace of blue stones on a thong. His fur skirt was similar to Girtab's, without the pockets for the knives.

Saj smiled releasing his forearm. "You called this meeting?"

"You'll see why when we get there."

"Do you have a new plan?"

"We need new ideas."

"Good. I have a few."

"How have you been doing?"

"I have a hundred and twenty men under my command."

"Very good."

"How's the slave trade?"

"Lucrative. I have some women for sale." He grinned at Saj.

Saj laughed. "I've already fathered five children. I've done my duty."

"Five that you know of."

"I was a soldier before the Lady rescued me, just like you."

"Yes, but I stayed with the soldiers."

"I didn't have much of a choice. I was married before going off to war."

Girtab waved a hand in dismissal. "Those are the old days. Now it's different."

"We still have a war to fight," said Saj.

"I'm glad you still know we have a war. Some of us ..."

Saj sighed. "Is this about Gud again?"

Girtab turned another corner and didn't answer.

"What is it about you two?"

They came upon the plaza that led to the White Temple of Ishtar. Saj almost put a hand to Girtab's shoulder to get him to stop, but Girtab turned around to him.

"We have a *duty.*"

"That doesn't mean he can't live a little."

Girtab glared, and then tossed his head back. "You'll see."

The men walked across the plaza to the ziggurat and entered one of the lower levels. It was getting dark, so someone was beginning to light torches through the hallway. They walked through the halls, Girtab knowing his way through, and Saj just a half-pace behind.

They came out into a small room, lit by torches. Two men were seated at a table full of food. One had his long hair pulled back by a white fabric headband and wore a robe decorated with tassels of fringe on it. He had a short, thick beard. The other was bald and wore a tunic similar to Saj, but much simpler.

"My brothers," said the man with the long hair, as he held his arms out. "Welcome, welcome."

"It's good to see you, Urmah," said Saj, clasping forearms with him. Girtab did also.

"You come here armed, Girtab?"

"It's for when I leave."

Said the other bald man, "I came with my spear and you didn't complain."

"Because," said Urmah, "You didn't hide your spear."

"Leave him alone," said Saj, as he took some cheese.

"Where is Gud?" asked Girtab.

"You know him," said the other bald man. "Late as usual."

"Hail to you all, blessings be upon your house," came a voice from the doorway. They all turned to see another bald man come in, wearing only a loincloth woven between his legs and pleated.

"Allul," cried Urmah, again holding his arms out. "Welcome!"

"Our Lady's grace upon you," said the bald man, as he kissed Urmah, and then each of the other men in turn. He stopped at Girtab, and put an arm around his waist. "Why are you angry?"

"Where is Gud?" he spat.

The rest of the men looked at him.

"Eat something," said Allul. "Because otherwise your anger will eat you up inside."

The bald man in the military tunic approached with a piece of bread and cheese. "He's right."

Girtab took the bread. Allul did not release Girtab's waist. "It's been so long since I've seen you."

"I've been busy."

"Too busy to come to my little hovel by the sea? You used to come there after every market day."

Then a man came into the room. Big and broad, he was built like a house. He filled the doorway. He smiled, beaming at them.

"Look what I have!"

He stepped aside, and a smaller man, with hair of flax and wearing only a loincloth like Allul stood in the doorway. He looked embarrassed.

Girtab drew himself to his full height. "Get that slave out of here."

"Slave?" said Urmah. "This meeting is for us only, not for any slaves."

"How do you know he's a slave?" asked Allul.

"Because I sold him to him two days ago," snarled Girtab. "Now get him out of here."

"He doesn't understand what you're saying," said Gud.

"Oh, he understands well enough!" said Girtab, as he approached the man.

He knew the man intimately because even he himself found him irresistible. Girtab didn't damage the goods, but he did take the slave to his bed to examine him thoroughly.

"We do not have slaves here," said Urmah firmly. "For very important reasons."

"Slaves gossip," said the other military man. "He's right. Bring him back home and come back."

"Send him upstairs until you're done," said Girtab. "I don't have time to wait all night while you reapply your makeup after you fuck him."

The big man narrowed his eyes at Girtab. "You're getting close."

Urmah slipped out of the room. Allul squeezed Girtab's waist to try and get him to calm down, because Girtab's entire body had gone rigid, preparing for a fight, at that one look from Gud.

The flaxen-haired young man did not move from the doorway, until two men in robes just like Urmah grabbed him and frog-marched him out of the room. He glanced back at Gud, a look of fear on his face.

Gud reassured him, "I'll come get you as soon as I'm done."

"Oh, he didn't understand that," said the military man.

"Shut up, Lahunga."

Lahunga just shrugged.

"Now, you see why I called this meeting," said Girtab, stepping out of Allul's embrace. "We drew lots, in the desert, when the Lady first called us back from the dead. Do you remember that?"

They all nodded.

"And you, Gud, drew the largest lot. And you, Gud, were going to be the one to land the killing blow on the Murderer." Girtab walked up to the big man, and stared up at him. "What have you done for three years?"

"Don't blame me —"

"Saj and Lahunga joined the military and have access to the palace as guards. Urmah became a priest of the

Lady and can go to the palace whenever he wishes. Allul is a fishmonger and has access to the palace kitchens. I am a slave-seller who can go to the palace at will with new slaves. And you, Gud? What access does a bullfighter have to the palace?"

"For your information, I have been working toward exactly that."

"Prove it."

"Gilgamesh has asked me to a banquet in honor of my defeating their Bull of Heaven." He looked to each of the men. "You will all come with me as my servants."

"Over my dead body," snarled Girtab.

"No," added Lahunga.

"I will go," said Allul.

"No," said Urmah. "I will not debase myself."

Everyone looked to Saj. Saj shrugged. "I am known in the Army now. If I go to a banquet disguised as a slave, they'll know me."

"That was a stupid idea!" Girtab said. "What happened to our original idea, that we would go into the palace under cover of night, and then we would go to his bedchamber and attack? How hard is that?"

"There are six of us. We won't be able to get through the cordon," said Lahunga.

"We can't die."

They looked at each other.

"You forget that, don't you? We live by the grace of the Lady, praise be Her name. If She chooses to claim us, then we will return to Erishkigal's realm willingly. We live our lives for Her."

"Then why are you in such a rush to get rid of it?" asked Gud.

Allul exhaled sharply, as if he'd been hit. Girtab rocked back. "We have ... a quest."

"You're so worried about the quest, did you ever think that the Lady gave us this life to live? We were taken too soon by that Murderer, and now we have a chance to live our lives again."

Saj said, "Let us ask the Lady what she wants of us."

Now all the heads turned to Urmah. He nodded.

"We will use the sacrificial temple. No one is there."

The six men followed Urmah up a set of winding stairs. He led them into a chamber, decorated with blue and white stones, showing the winged bulls in relief. At the end of the chamber was a figure of a woman, her eyes painted black, her black hair long past her shoulders. This was an older temple than the ones above, and meant for smaller gatherings. The altar was unlit, though it would be for the private use of those who meant to sacrifice.

The six men disrobed, hanging their clothes on hooks located outside of the chamber. Even Urmah took off his fringed robes. Girtab nodded, remembering far back to his childhood when his mother took him to Innana a long time ago: "All are naked before the gods, for all are equal in their eyes."

They crowded into the hot room, dimly lit by one torch and a high window to the outside. Urmah began the chant, the hymn to the goddess, and the men joined in one by one as each line was sung. Girtab swayed with the men, with the music of their voices, finding himself in a half-trance.

The altar fires burst forth. Urmah stepped back, bumping into the men behind him. He stared, wide-eyed into the flame. Then it dampened, and slowly went out. He turned to face the men.

"Well?" asked Girtab.

"We attack. Tonight."

Gud stammered, "I'm not ready!"

Urmah said coldly, "You will be."

The rest of the men exited the small chamber, and quietly got dressed. They were soldiers now, and they had their orders.

"You've gotten soft with your easy living," said Girtab. "Was she angry with us?"

Urmah shook his head. "We are to attack him now, that's all she said. I will get robes for us all, to go to the palace." He turned to Gud. "And a sword, for you."

They all followed Urmah again to another chamber. Here were weapons, and each of the men selected some. Saj, a bow, but Luhunga kept his spear. Girtab took the throwing knives out of his fur skirt. Allul took two short swords. Gud looked through the weapons without choosing one. Urmah returned, his arms full of robes. He plucked a sword off the wall and shoved it at Gud.

Gud made a noise, something like fear, and took the blade. Allul took a robe, and put it on. Girtab took a robe, and the rest took theirs, Gud taking his last.

"Now we go," said Urmah.

He led them out of the chambers, down a couple of stairs, to the base of the ziggurat. They crossed the plaza to the palace, and walked through the gate. They were let inside without anyone stopping them.

It wasn't until they got into the courtyard inside the palace that they didn't know where to go. Saj looked up at the sky, and pointed down the hall. "In there."

They walked in a single line toward the entrance. They all kept their hands near the blades or at the ready as they walked in single file through the halls, passing exposed chambers. Saj led, an arrow nocked.

He turned another corner and stepped aside. Urmah went into the room. The rest of the men spread out in the room, and saw two large men, Gilgamesh with Enkidu, both alone in the bath.

No guards. No women. No weapons.

All six men at the same time bared their weapons. Gilgamesh turned toward them. "What is —"

With a roar, Gud raised his sword and went at Gilgamesh. At the same time, Saj let loose an arrow, Girtab a throwing blade. Both hit a mark, but not the mark that was meant, because Enkidu stepped between Gilgamesh, the rushing man and the weapons.

The sword bit deep into Enkidu's neck and shoulder. The arrow pierced his other shoulder, while the blade caught the right side of his breast. Luhunga rushed forward with his spear, and impaling Enkidu through his side.

Seeing that they had not hit Gilgamesh, Girtab took aim again, this time at Gilgamesh's neck, and threw the blade. He watched with disbelief as the blade changed its trajectory, all on its own, and slammed into the neck of Enkidu.

Urmah turned around to face the guards that were coming into the chamber. Girtab, knowing something was stopping him from killing Gilgamesh, turned and fought side by side with Urmah. Allul, a whirling mass of swords, sliced through the guards.

Saj was the first one to say it: "I can't hit him!"

Gilgamesh got out of the bloody bath as Gud went toward him again. This time, Gilgamesh was ready, and dodged out of the way of the swinging blade. "Go out, go out!" yelled Urmah.

Luhunga retrieved his spear, and held it before him. Like a machine, Saj sent arrows off into the crowd of guards at the door, who went down like wheat.

"Gud!"

"I will kill you!" Gud roared, and went at Gilgamesh again. Girtab turned back around to see Gilgamesh grab Gud and throw him into the pool. The robe took on water, and Gilgamesh jumped back into the bloody mess.

Saj yelled, "It's clear, let's GO."

"We're not leaving Gud!" cried Girtab, starting to head back.

Gilgamesh had grabbed Gud by the hair and shoved him head first into the pool.

"OUT, NOW!" yelled Luhunga, shoving Girtab through the doorway. They ran at a breakneck speed down some hallways; Saj leading the way to the palace's outer edge and the water.

"Allul!" Saj called.

Allul came forward. He looked out into the night, then said, "I see one."

He ran down toward the edge of the stairs, and there was a moored boat. Allul undid the ties while Urmah jumped into the boat. They heard the noise of the palace awakening, lights being lit throughout it.

When everyone was on the boat, Allul put his hand in the water. A great rush of water came from his hand, and the boat pushed away from the palace steps. Girtab stared up at the palace as the boat jerked out into the Euphrates.

"Gud is dead," said Urmah, "May the Lady accept Her to Her bosom again."

"Gud can't be dead," said Luhunga. "Only the Lady takes us in death. So She promised."

"I've drowned numerous times," said Allul, as he let the boat lazily drift downriver. "It isn't pleasant, but I haven't died."

"This is all my fault," said Girtab, staring at the bottom of the boat.

"Yes," said Saj, "It is."

"That's why you're going to stop him from getting buried alive." Lahunga said.

Girtab looked to his brothers. None looked sympathetic to him; this meant he was going to have to do this alone.

$$\Delta$$

Allul brought them downstream to the wharf where he lived. They all disembarked, and he sent the boat to drift further downstream, where it would either be picked up by someone else or break up in the water.

Knowing they were now in the area of Ur where walking the streets at night meant you took your life in your own hands, they all switched to have their arms at hand.

"Guards will be walking the streets of the upper city," said Allul.

"It's best if we stay around here for tonight," said Saj.

Lahunga sighed. "Looks like we're not getting any sleep."

"I wasn't planning on it," said Urmah. "I was planning on getting away. I can't go back to the temple."

"Did you see what happened to our weapons?" said Girtab. "They didn't touch the Murderer, but they —"

Allul made a hissing sound. Girtab fell silent.

"My home is among others. I will give you clothes, Urmah, but you must stay here."

"We'll return to the army," said Saj, looking at Luhunga, who nodded.

Girtab said, "I guess I have a job to do. I'll do it as soon as I take care of the slaves I have for auction tomorrow."

"Of course, make your money before saving our brother," snarled Saj.

"He's right," Allul said. "We must return to our jobs so that no one knows."

Luhunga said, "We need to return to the army before first light, Saj."

Saj glared at Girtab, a look of near hatred on his face. Then he turned from the group and strode out into the night, Luhunga jumping to follow him.

Allul turned to Urmah. "I will find a boat for you and we will go fishing this morning."

Urmah frowned.

Allul laughed and put his arm around Urmah's shoulders. "Come, I will make you feel better about it."

Girtab knew what that meant, from knowing Allul in the past. Allul would let Urmah have his way with him. Knowing what Allul would do made him stir under the robes. But he didn't have time to do that now.

He had to go back home and be ready for sunrise when the markets would open.

Δ

"Five bushels of barley from the man in the center."

The man in the center nodded. He stepped up and placed in Girtab's hand five bronze coins. Girtab was the third slaver today and had just finished selling off the last of his wares. He usually stuck around to try and buy other slaves, and then resell them later, or find particular slaves for certain patrons.

One of the young boys who frequented the upper city said that a traitor was captured and he was going to be put out in the desert. He had also heard that Enkidu, Gilgamesh's best friend, was found dead last night, and Gilgamesh was beside himself with grief. Some reports said he was killed defending Gilgamesh, others that he died of wounds suffered during the melee. Some said that the traitor did it; some said that a hundred men attacked the palace. All of them said that Gilgamesh wanted the whole city to go into mourning. As with all the slavers and all the workers, they waited for an actual decree from the palace. In the meantime, business went on as usual. For Girtab, he was going to go out into the desert and find his brother, and they would escape Ur together. Where they would go, he didn't know, but he did know that they weren't going to be able to kill Gilgamesh again.

What would the Goddess think of his cowardice? Would She strike him down? He deserved it, after all.

He travelled to the upper city, his heart heavy, just in time to see the cage containing Gud get pulled through the streets. People threw things at him. He had nothing to cover himself, but he stood proudly and let the objects hit him. Girtab could see thick welts across Gud's back — he had been whipped before being placed in the cage. A stone struck his head and God stumbled against the cage. People roared and threw even more things at him. Rotten food, excrement, stones — whatever came to hand.

"My brother," Girtab whispered, as the cage rattled down the street, heading toward the desert gate. Girtab fought his way through the crowd until he got to the desert gate, where the crowd was too thick to get through. Here, people yelled instead of threw things. "Igibala, Igibala!" *Traitor, traitor!* "Ludaku!" *Murderer!*

Girtab fought back tears as the cage went through the gate and people crowded around it, while guards stopped them from following it out. They didn't want other people to find him and possibly set him free. They would put him deep into the desert, and then return by nightfall.

Girtab watched the cage turn into a shimmering mirage and disappear over the dunes. It was late in the afternoon, and he found that he was hungry. But he would not eat — he would suffer like his brother was going to suffer. He would drink to keep his strength up, but he would fast for his brother.

Milling around the upper city, Girtab avoided guards and looked at merchant wares. He bought a large warm robe for Gud when he would release him. Three skins of beer he also bought, two to carry, and one to drink from throughout the day.

Girtab also avoided the temple to Ishtar, thought he wanted to go into it and pray for guidance and help. He paid a priest to make a sacrifice of a lamb for him instead.

The afternoon wore on, until finally it was nightfall. He stayed at the gate, waiting until the men who had taken the cage returned. He would follow them back into the city, and maybe ply one or two with some beer at a food stall to get an idea of what direction they went.

"Slaver, what are you doing here?"

He turned to face a guard. Girtab only smiled. "I am waiting for my next shipment."

"From here? Other slavers usually receive their goods from the gates."

"I'm holding a spot."

"You've been hanging around most of the day. You were expecting them?"

"Since this morning."

The guard frowned. "You should not stay here."

"Let me stay until dark."

"Fine."

Girtab let out a breath. Lies, but he had to tell them. Lies came easily to him at times, and this was one of them.

Eventually, in the distance, he saw men riding asses toward them. He waited until they came back, and then he followed them toward the palace. Girtab got a good look at them when they came in and memorized their faces.

Near the palace were some food stalls that were open late at night for the soldiers and guards. Girtab hung around there as well. Then full dark fell, and the men at the food stalls started packing up for the night.

A man bumped into Girtab, hard. He turned to look at him to give him a piece of his mind and saw that it was Luhunga. He said, cryptically, "Follow the sun until it is straight up above you."

That meant he needed to go northwest. Girtab said nothing, but slunk back into the night. He did not go back to his home. He stayed with a holy prostitute in the temple of Ishtar, hoping for a dream.

After he performed his necessary act — he imagined that it was the Goddess that he was making love to, and the girl made too much noise — he settled down to sleep. He saw his brothers, each one: Saj asleep in his barracks, Luhunga on guard, Allul and Urmah entwined together on a straw pallet in Allul's humble home. Last he saw Gud, in the cage, trying to sleep but shivering in the dark. Girtab moved closer to Gud, and put his hand on Gud's shoulder.

Gud woke up, startled, then stared in the dark. "What are you doing here?"

"I'm sorry," he said. "This is all my fault."

Gud looked down. "No, it's mine. I shouldn't have gotten used to my life. I should have kept my eye on what we were there for."

"I will come come tomorrow to save you."

"And then what? I can't go back to Ur."

"We'll have to go somewhere else. Find a village and live out our days."

"If the Lady will let us. We live on Her whim."

Girtab knew that. It was a chance they were going to have to take. The brothers would be separated, possibly forever.

"Come get me," said Gud. "Please."

Girtab lost his hold on Gud, and he came back to himself, back to the pallet where the prostitute lay with him.

He remembered looking at Gud, his mountainous body, and thought of him taking him in "punishment", ...

He groaned, turned and got up. The prostitute reached for him, but he shook her off. "No, I need to go."

She said nothing more as she got up and put her robe on. "The Lady blesses you."

"I hope so," he said, and left the temple.

The sun was coming up, and he went to the desert gate. He had the robe, refilled his beer skin, and headed out into the desert alone.

He walked, heading northwest, following the sun as it traversed across the sky.

He trudged through the desert. A lone man, walking through the desert looked like a suicide. There were animals in the desert, not only those of his namesake, but other animals that would attack him without any warning.

Then there were also bandits.

He should have taken a horse or an ass.

He crested a hill, and saw before him just desert, but in the distance he could see something other than the mirage. He looked up at the sun, and kept walking, since it wasn't above him. He finally came down into a bowl, and climbed down into it, then up at the other side. At the top, he saw the first box.

This box was old and had been broken apart. Inside was a human skeleton, or the remains of one. He looked out, and saw that boxes and cages were scattered all around — here was the graveyard of traitors, adultresses, thieves, left to the mercy of the desert.

The boxes had thieves, some obelisks existed too — these were the adultresses. Traitors were exposed to the elements, so that they would never rest.

He took a sip of beer and walked through the graveyard, checking inside the cages to see skeletons, decomposing bodies. A skinny wolf was worrying at a corpse in one of the cages. The wolf didn't even look up at him.

"Gud!" he yelled.

"Over here!" he heard.

He tried to follow the voice. He kept calling for him, listening to the response, checking all the cages. Finally, he saw a man standing in a cage, and he ran toward it. "Gud!"

Gud was naked in the cage, staying away from the bars which were hot in the sun. "Girtab," he called, his voice hoarse.

Girtab first handed over the wine skin of beer. Gud drank slowly while Girtab put the robe in the cage. Next, he looked at the lock. It had been snapped cleanly.

"You broke it."

"Last night."

Gud pulled on the robe and pushed open the door, his hand covered over with part of the robe. "Where are we going now?"

"To the caves," said Girtab. "We'll have to chase out the bandits that are there."

"That won't be too difficult."

Girtab looked out into the desert. "We have to get there, first."

As it happened, the caves came to them.

Δ

They walked out of the graveyard and into the desert, heading toward the caves, when Gud said, "There's dust."

Thinking it was a dust storm, Girtab looked frantically for somewhere where they could get some cover. "Run this way, maybe we can outrun it."

They ran west, heading toward scrubland instead of the mountains. The storm followed them. Gud paused and looked out at the storm. "Girtab, it's bandits."

Girtab stopped, panting, and peered. Black riders were at the base of the dust, which lessened as they got into the scrubland. They had no weapons.

They stood their ground.

The bandits galloped up to them, five of them, their horses breathing heavily in the heat. One of them had a spear, which he pointed at Girtab. Girtab thrust his chest out, as if daring him to impale him.

"Escaped from the grave," said one man, holding onto a prancing horse. He had a thick beard and his eyes were black coals. "What do you think about having a new life?"

"Thought about it," said Gud. "Are there slaves?"

The man laughed, "Only the ones that you choose to make your slaves. And you must be strong."

"I am strong," said Gud. "The strongest man alive."

"Even stronger than Gilgamesh, that evil ruler?"

"I would have been," he said. "I was strong enough to kill Enkidu."

"The ruler's bedmate," said the man. "Do you repudiate your ties to that city? Will you live your life out as a member of my band? For they have done nothing for you."

Girtab thought about it. They wouldn't have to go very far, and they would be fed on the rich men of the city who dared to try and pass through to the city.

"Yes," said Girtab. "Yes, I do."

Gud said sadly, "But my slave?"

"Let it go, he's been sold to someone else by this time, as has all of your property."

"I want my gold-haired slave."

"We'll get him in due time," said Girtab, and looked up at the man on the horse. "We will join you."

"Good, because otherwise, I would have had to kill you. Can you ride?"

Gud shook his head. Girtab nodded.

One of the men dismounted and helped Gud get onto the horse, while Girtab easily mounted another man's horse. They rode back slowly, so as to not put any undue strain on the animals carrying two.

Δ

Time passed. Months, then years. Girtab watched Gud gather slaves to him, but he always pined for that flaxen-haired young man. Many bandits took females to rape and then sent them back, but others took boys or men. So it wasn't surprising if Girtab went to Gud's bed, or if Gud went to Girtab.

Yet Girtab also watched Gud lose his strength. They learned quickly how to ride, but as the years went by, Girtab watched as Gud grew older, his hair graying, and his eyes losing their sight.

Girtab kept looking in pools of water to see if he also aged, but he had not. Bandit leaders came and went, defeated or killed by other, younger men. Girtab never took the reins of leadership, though many wanted him to; it was enough that he took care of his own. Gud eventually got too old and sore to sit a horse. Usually the bandits would have turned him out, sent him back into the city. Girtab took him as his own, and no one denied him that.

Then, one day, Gud did not wake up.

With tears in his eyes, Girtab had men take him out to bury him. He distributed his own wealth among his friends, and took a horse to head back to Ur.

When he got there, he noticed the walls had fallen into disrepair, and not half as many men were lining it. He was allowed to enter without a challenge.

The square where the markets had been was deserted. He nudged his horse down to the wharfs, and saw that the bustling business that had been while he was there had turned into a trickle. He went to Allul's shack, and found it gone.

He turned his horse around and headed back into the city, toward the temple of Ishtar. There, the prostitutes were old and ugly, and there were only a few priests. No one sold offerings outside of the temple, and he had only coin, which the Lady Ishtar did not like.

He went into the cool, dark temple, finding his way to the main prayer chamber, where the statue of Ishtar was there, but no priests. The fire at her feet had dwindled to embers.

She? Even she has left? He knelt with one knee and bowed his head.

"Lady, I beg of you, where have the people gone?"

Thy Brothers are scattered among the winds.

He stared wide-eyed at the floor. Something spoke, directly to him, filling his mind.

Gud has returned to the palace of Erishkigal and his eyes set as stars. But he shall return. Thou shalt live until thou finds my love in another man's eyes. Men will need thee, and thou shalt have power to guide thee.

"Yes, my Lady," he whispered, his eyes full of wonder and tears. He remembered the love she bore him, and could feel it now in this room. He got up and broke the rules by walking up to the statue. He hugged her leg, tears of love and desire flowing now, tears of his want of Her and of his brothers.

CANCER

SEPTEMBER 18, 1932
SOUTHERN KANSAS

I

THE MAN WHO CALLED HIMSELF DAN GOLD stood around St. Mary's Mission, looking for work. He had taken the train from Topeka, after hearing that the farmers here hired day laborers.

Dan stood an easy five-eight, with auburn hair and light blue eyes. Based on his size, he could have been drafted into the War To End All Wars, but his father made sure that he didn't have to go, paying off some people somewhere in New York. He had a bit of scruffy beard growing so he looked younger than his twenty-two years.

At St. Mary's, he followed the crowd of men from farmer to farmer. He had a cloth bag with his clothes in it, though he wore the same clothes he came to Kansas with four days ago. The other clothes in the bag were clean, folded neatly, and packed with care.

Farmers filled their trucks with workers for the harvest, for work around the farms — anywhere that needed a day laborer. One farmer, in a set of denim overalls and a checkered shirt, stood in the back of an old Ford truck that had seen better days. No one stood at his truck, but four sullen men sat in the back. The number of men gathered around had dwindled to five or six, and none of them came up to the farmer. Dan didn't understand why.

The farmer waved him over. "You, come on."

The farmer helped Dan with his bag while he jumped into the truck. Dan nodded to the other men in greeting. The other men didn't look happy.

"Good," said the farmer. "Hope you're willing to work, boys."

"What's the pay?" asked one man.

"Five dollars for today," said the farmer.

Two of the men whistled. "That's a lot," said one.

"What're we gonna be doing?" asked the first man.

"Baling, mostly," the farmer said. The farmer jumped down off the back of the truck. As he pulled out of the mission, he slammed on his brakes and almost threw Dan over the side. The horse and wagon driver who cut him off yelled something incoherent at them. The farmer did nothing, but took a different way out of the mission.

"What's your name, boy?" asked the man seated next to Dan.

He was one of the men who whistled at the pay. He was slightly heavyset, with brown hair and big callused hands. He had a round face, not like the other men who looked to Dan like weasels, with pointed chins and noses.

"Dan," he said. "Yours?"

"Mitch." They shook hands. "You're not from around here?" Mitch motioned to the bag between Dan's feet.

"No."

"Where ya from?"

"New York City."

"New York City? Why'd you leave there?"

"My parents wanted me to marry someone."

"Did you get her knocked up?"

"No," he said looking away. "No, it was an arranged marriage."

"No shit. They still do that?"

"In my family, they do."

Said another man, "Sounds like a buncha greenhorns."

Dan looked down, a little embarrassed.

The other men talked among themselves about the weather. It had been hot, without a cloud in the sky in St. Mary's, hot enough to dry out the grass and prepare it for haying. The truck eventually turned off Military Road and headed down what seemed to be a glorified cow path. Even more bumpy, it made conversation difficult as the men held onto the edge of the truck.

Surrounding Dan was field after field of uncut grass. His shoulders slumped. They would be here all day with a sickle taking this all down. With a less than a dozen men? Probably all week.

The truck parked next to a barn that needed painting and the farmer put on the brake. Dan jumped down, grabbing his bag, while the rest jumped out of the truck around him. The farmer got out of the truck, and with a "Follow me, boys," started bringing them to the other side of the barn.

"Already did the raking, now comes the fun part."

The men groaned, all except Dan, who didn't know what he was in for.

The farmer looked at Dan. "You wanna set that somewhere?" He pointed to the bag.

"Yes," Dan said.

He looked around, putting it in one of the stables, hiding it behind the door. The men had already gone outside to a boxy wagon being pulled by a chestnut brown horse.

The farmer took off his hat for a moment. He had very short black hair. He had thick muscles leading from his shoulders to his neck. His shoulders were broad, and Dan could see the muscles defined in his forearms. His bicep flexed through the thin, threadbare cotton shirt. Dan glanced at his groin and could see a large muscle there.

He jerked his head up as the farmer looked directly at him. "You ever done this before, boy?"

"Er, no."

"Then you'll haul up. You two stack," he pointed to Mitch and another man. "You pitch," he pointed to a smaller man, not much more than a boy, "and you tie."

"How much hay are we talking here?" asked Mitch.

The farmer laughed, "Boys, we're gonna be doing this 'til at least sundown."

"Shit, I gotta be home for the wife then."

The farmer pointed to the path. "Go back that way, then. I ain't got all day."

The man looked back and forth, between leaving and staying, and then climbed into the box of the wagon. The rest of the men followed suit. The wagon then went out into the fields.

They went to a different field than the one Dan had seen from the road. In this field were large piles of grass, taller than the wagon. Another flat wagon was already there.

The farmer stopped the box-wagon. He dug out two pitchforks, and handed one to one of the weaselly men. Then the farmer and the weasel climbed to the top of the pile of grass and started shovelling it into the box. When it was full, the boy tied it off, and shoved it out of the box to Dan's feet. Dan picked up the bale of hay and carried it to the flat wagon, tossing it there. Mitch took the bale and stacked it against the back of the flat wagon.

Dan was not used to the work. It was hot, the bales were heavy, and he fell behind often. The farmer undid his shirt, and Dan tried not to stare at the man as he worked. In what seemed like forever, there was nothing left of the pile of hay. The farmer unhitched the horse from the box-wagon to the flat wagon, and also carried a large barrel to the flat wagon. He ladled out water, first to the horse, then to the men. Dan drank like a man who had spent months in the desert.

"Not used to this, are you, son?" asked the farmer kindly.

"No," said Dan, looking embarrassed again. His hands hurt, his shoulders hurt — everything about him hurt.

The farmer said, "You, boy, switch with this boy here."

They drove to the next pile of hay, pulling the hay bailer along with them. The farmer worked right alongside them. Dan found that he was good at the shovelling and the tying off, once he got the hang of it. When the sun was high in the sky, beating down on them, they drove the full flat wagon back to the barn.

They had a light lunch, sandwiches that had some mysterious spread on the inside. He loved it, and asked what it was. "Deviled ham," said the farmer.

Dan stared at the sandwich. Well, there was no use for it. He couldn't ask for anything else. He finished it.

They unloaded the bales of hay in the barn, just stacking them against one of the walls, and went back out into the field. They rotated their positions, tossing hay in the bailer, packing it down, tying it off, shooting it out at someone's feet, and they picked it up and brought it to the wagon, who laid it up against the side. They worked in silence.

When the men finished, the sun was setting. They brought the wagon back to the barn but didn't unload it. The farmer unhitched the horse, putting it in the stable. He spoke to it softly, and the horse went to its trough, drinking the water.

As the men got one last drink of water, the farmer returned, and handed each of them a five-note. "I'll drive you back to St. Mary's."

Dan, for his part, could barely stand. He had taken the money, shoving it in his pocket without thinking and then half-tumbled into the back of the truck. He was tired, hungry, stank like a pig, and wanted to crawl into a bath or a bed.

The other men looked just as tired.

"Never worked so hard for five dollars in my life," complained Mitch. "No wonder they told me not to work for him."

"They who?" asked Dan.

Mitch waved a hand absently. "My wife's family. 'He pays good money, but you work like a dog' they said."

The men didn't dare fall asleep, afraid they would fall out of the truck, so it was a hair-raising ride in the twilight back to St. Mary's mission. When they got there, they all moaned getting out of the truck. Dan slipped and fell, hitting his side on the bumper.

The farmer helped him up. "You need help?" he asked.

"No," Dan murmured, struggling to his feet. Did he bruise a rib?

He stumbled like a drunken man to the hostel in town. There, he could probably get a bath, maybe a bed. All he needed was —

He stopped, patted his pockets like he had forgotten something. He stuck his hand in his pocket and came out with a five-dollar silver note. No, that wasn't it. He shrugged slightly and continued to the hostel.

It was crowded with people when he entered and went to the desk. The elderly matron turned her nose up at him and said all the rooms were full. At this point, he thought, he'd sleep in the middle of the street. He turned around, and bumped right into the farmer.

"Oh, I thought you went in here. You had a bag, didn't you?"

"Yes, I did," Dan said, suddenly realizing what he forgotten. "I'll pick it up tomorrow."

"I won't be here tomorrow," said the farmer. "You can come back to my place and sleep there. I have plenty of room."

Dan shrugged again. "What'll it cost me?"

"We can discuss that on the way."

Dan followed the farmer outside, stumbling down the steps. The farmer caught him and put his arm around him, keeping him steady until they got to his truck. Dan didn't even remember getting placed gently in the front seat and falling asleep.

2

Dan heard the slam of a steel door and jerked awake, looking around in a panic. He sat in the cab of a truck, the sun coming up through the windshield.

"Rise and shine!"

Standing at the hood was the farmer, a grin on his face. He wore no shirt, clothed in worn blue dungarees. Dan stared at the man's chest. He had black hair in the middle and down his abdomen. His abdomen and sides had deep, cut lines.

Dan rubbed his eyes. "I slept in here?"

"Like a baby," said the farmer. "I didn't want to disturb you. I think if a train ran through here you never would have noticed."

Looking out the window past the man, Dan saw a white farmhouse with a wrap-around porch, many windows, and two floors. It looked like it had been weather-beaten and some shutters were missing. To his left, about 300 yards away, was the barn.

"Want some breakfast?"

"Uh, yes," Dan said, squirming uncomfortably. He opened the door and slid out.

"Outhouse is that way," said the farmer, thumbing toward the rear of the house. "Name's Rack, by the way."

"Dan," he said, shaking the man's big hand as he walked by. Rack held on a little longer than he should have, and then let him go. Dan walked away, feeling strange.

Dan used the outhouse and saw that there was a back door to the house. He tried it, and it let him into a kitchen. The ice box was to the side of the sink, along with a wood stove next to the door. He could see the entrance way into a large dining area. Rack was standing at the table, holding two plates. "Eat up, we got a lot of work to do."

"We?"

Rack chuckled, "I'm not letting you go, now that I have you. Don't worry. I'll still pay you a day's wage."

Dan sat down. The dining area looked bare of anything decorative, like doilies, photographs, pictures on the walls. On a small table to the side held a dried starfish and some seashells on it.

Dan sat down. On the plate were three fried eggs, biscuits, sausage and gravy. He'd never had this before, and wasn't sure how to eat it. He watched Rack take some toast and dip it into the yolk of the egg. He did the same thing. It wasn't bad.

Rack asked, "So tell me, what's a city boy like you doing so far west?"

Dan swallowed, drank some of the coffee. It was strong enough that he shuddered. Rack chuckled.

"So?"

"I'm trying to make a life for myself."

"By being a farmhand?"

"I didn't want to stay in the city."

"You're running away."

Dan sipped the coffee again.

"From what?"

Dan shrugged. "My parents want me to get married. Settle down."

"And you don't."

"I don't want to get married. I see what it's doing to my sister." He glanced up at Rack. "Her husband hits her."

Rack pursed his lips.

"But he comes from a good family. He's a doctor. He knows what he's doing. My sister, well, she can be a shrew."

"You're afraid you'll hit your wife?"

He said nothing for a moment.

Rack sat back in the chair. "You're afraid she'll hit *you*."

Dan turned red, staring at his plate. "She's used to getting what she wants. She's very rich, and likes rich things. I don't."

"You're a simple man. You aren't the type of man to run around putting women in their places."

He shook his head still looking down. "I don't … "

"You don't like women," Rack said quietly, as he went back to eating. "We don't need to talk about it."

Dan stared at him, blinking. How did he know? How could he tell?

Rack paused for a moment and looked at Dan. "I'm a good reader of people." He motioned to the plate. "Hurry up, it's getting cold."

"You live alone?" Dan asked while he ate.

"Yep."

"Why?"

He shrugged. "People don't like me much."

Dan remembered what the farmhand had said. "Is it because of all the work you make people do?"

"Maybe."

Rack scooped up the rest of his eggs, picked up his plate, and went into the kitchen. Dan hurried and finished, then brought his plate into the kitchen. Rack took it from him and started to wash it. Dan could see no spigots for the water. No indoor plumbing?

"We'll start with the barn. Horses need mucking out; cows need to be put out. Already took care of the hen house. Hay needs to be stacked in the barn. Garden needs harvesting. Then I'll go to town, drop you off." He finished washing and set the plates on the rack to dry.

"I thought you said you were going to keep me."

"Now you want to stay?" Rack grinned, plucked a shirt off of a hook behind the door. "You gotta do one thing, though."

"What's that?"

"Take a bath every night."

"Agreed," Dan said with a laugh and held out his hand.

Rack shook it firmly. "Horses," he said, pulling on his shirt and walking out.

They put the horses and cows out in two separate pastures and then cleaned out the stables, putting down fresh hay. "If you're going to stay, I'm cleaning the barn before the next frost," Rack said.

Dan could only pant. Then they stacked the bales of hay into the loft. Rack used a pulley and winch. While Dan hooked the hay, Rack pulled it up. He swung it into the loft and stacked it there.

For lunch, they had the same deviled ham again. After that, they went to the garden. It was wide enough to push wheelbarrow between the rows. Dan pushed the barrow while Rack did most of the harvesting. He clucked a few times, seeing things that had rotted. He tossed them on the ground and dug them beneath the soil. They filled about half of the wheelbarrow. Rack took the root vegetables and put those in the cellar for storage, and brought the more perishable up to the kitchen. For supper, they had cucumbers and tomatoes along with a sandwich with sliced beef tongue.

On a swinging bench on the porch, Dan sat on it alone, dozing off, while Rack watched the fireflies in the twilight. A wagon with two men started up the path toward the house.

Rack went to the railing of the porch. *"Bozho nikan!"* he called.

"Bozho Kmowin," replied the man who wasn't driving. He smiled and waved, jumping down as soon as the wagon stopped. Dan saw from his coloring and his face that he wasn't a white man — he was an Indian.

After grasping forearms, Rack motioned to Dan. "Kewankah, this is Dan."

"Dan," he said, and held out his hand. Dan went to shake, but the man grasped his forearm instead and squeezed. *"Bozho nikan."*

"Uh, bozo nikan to you too."

The Indian laughed. "We speak English too, friend. That is my cousin, Nakobee." Nakobee waved, not looking in their direction. The Indian looked to Rack. "Kmowin, it has been over a week."

Rack leaned out over the railing and looked at the sky. "Yes, it has. Do you have everything you need?"

"We were waiting for you," he said.

"I just got finished yesterday." Rack pondered, then shrugged. "If the rest of them didn't finish: the hell with them. I gave them plenty of time."

"Good, good! You will come to the dance tomorrow, then?"

"I will be happy to go. If I can bring my friend," he inclined his head toward Dan.

"Yes, bring him!" Kewankah bumped Dan's shoulder with his own. "There will be many pretty girls."

Dan refrained from rolling his eyes.

"He's already taken care of," Rack said.

"I can tell." He waved his hand in front of his face. "Have you been playing in manure?"

Dan had worn these clothes for five days now and he had been working hard. "I'm sorry," he said. "I've been working."

"You have. I know white men do not like water, but you should go to the creek."

Rack glared. "Be nice to my guest. He's going to have a bath after this."

Kewankah looked at Dan. "I'm sorry."

Dan flushed a deep red of embarrassment. "I'll go take it now." Before anyone could say anything, he went to the barn.

Taking out his bag, he opened it and could smell his mother's cooking. He missed his mother. And his father. And even the cousins who were always underfoot. Then he thought about Rebecca, the fat whining girl — how his mother had told him what a good match she'd be. How his father gave him the ticket to get on the train to Boston, telling him to be nice to the Mendelsons. How he got off at the next stop, threw his yarmulke over the side of the tracks, took the money his mother gave him and bought a ticket as far west as he could go with it ... which brought him here.

He took out the five-dollar silver certificate and put it in the pocket of his new black pants. All he had left were his black clothes — clothing he was expected to wear in Boston. He would have to wash the clothes he wore to stay incognito. He wondered if he should send his parents a post or something, Once they found out from the Mendelsons that he never got there, they would be worried.

"I can spare a bit for a post card," said Rack as he came into the barn.

Dan got up and turned around. "You've been doing that to me all day."

"What?" Rack tried to look innocent.

"Telling me what I'm thinking."

"You're an easy person to read, Dan. If that's your real name."

He looked at his clothes. "No."

"Daniel?"

"Jordan," he said.

Rack came up to him and put his hand on Dan's shoulder. "Jordan what?"

"Jordan Goldblum."

"I'll still call you Dan, if that's all right with you."

Dan nodded. "Please," he said.

"You're not only running away from your marriage, but you're running away from your life, your family. You want to make a new life here."

"Stop it," Dan said, throwing his clothes down and glaring at Rack. "Stop telling me what I'm thinking!"

"I'm sorry."

He let Dan's shoulder go. Dan reached up with his other hand and took Rack's hand. Rack's hand was calloused and rough from work. Is this what he had to look forward to?

Rack laid his hand gently back on Dan's shoulder. Dan pulled on Rack's hand, pulling it down lower. Rack looked intently into Dan's eyes.

Dan saw that Rack's eyes were black, not even a dark brown. Those eyes were a window into his soul. Dan saw that Rack had lived a hard life, alone, out here on the prairie. He lived a hard live, period. Dan wanted to ease that, to help him. He started to lean forward, his eyes closed, preparing to kiss those succulent lips.

Rack leaned forward also, and their lips met, for one shocking moment. They parted. Rack and Dan stared at each other. Then both men, at the same time, grabbed each other by the back of the head and pulled toward each other.

Dan had never been kissed like this. He'd kissed girls, but they were dainty and sweet, not like this. Not with underlying power and passion. The whole experience took his breath away.

They parted again. Both men panted, and moved away from each other. Rack spoke first. "I - "

Dan said at the same time, "I - "

They both laughed.

"I'm going to bring in the animals," Rack said with a last caress of Dan's chin. "You take a bath."

Dan found the bathtub in the stained-glass window room directly opposite the foyer. The water in it was warm, not hot, and he slid into it. He found a bar of soap was on the shelf above the bathtub, so he used that to wash the dirt, grime, and sweat off him. Then he sat while until he turned into a prune and the water got too cold. By then, he heard the door open and leaned forward to see Rack come in.

The sun had gone down; the house was dim. Dan watched as Rack stripped off all his clothes in the foyer, leaving them in a basket by the door. He padded into the room.

"Oh, I thought you would have been done by now."

Dan felt himself get rock hard at seeing Rack naked. He was a walking vision of muscles and tendons and veins, all perfectly formed, shaped, and uncut. Dan watched as Rack started to swell under his gaze.

Dan moved in the water, getting to his knees in the tub. Some primal instinct ... something took over and wanted him to do this. He brought his hand out of the cool water and cupped Rack's manhood in his hand. He hefted its weight, feeling its thickness, the vein underneath, the ridges, and how his foreskin pulled back from the glistening head.

Rack hissed. "Dan," he said, almost a growl. "Have you ever —"

Dan breathed on the man's large cock, then kissed it, and licked his lips, tasting the salty brine of the man.

"No," he whispered. "But I want to."

Rack placed his hand on Dan's wet hair. Dan kissed it again, and then his tongue snaked out, licking it. It was so hot, so smooth.

Rack's hand clenched on Dan's head. "You're teasing me."

"Should I stop?"

He kissed and licked him again, tasting him.

"No," whispered Rack.

Dan licked more, flicking his tongue along the smooth head. "Am I doing this right?"

"God, yes," Rack moaned.

Then Dan finally took him in his mouth and Rack tensed. Dan pulled his head back quickly.

"No, no, I almost ... damn."

"You almost did? Want me to do that again?"

Rack only nodded, and Dan did do it again.

Rack tensed, clenching Dan's hair. Dan moved his head up and down, trying to take all of him. Instead, he wrapped his hand around the last three inches, and only moved his head.

Rack said, "Stop, stop."

Dan froze. Gently, Rack pushed Dan off of him, and he stroked himself, looking at Dan.

"Oh ... gods ..." he moaned, and grunted. He came, all over Dan's chest, showering him in white ribbons.

Rack looked down, a broad smile on his face. After a moment, he bent down, and picked Dan up out of the water, as if he weighed nothing. Carrying him in a bridal carry, he brought him upstairs. As he walked, Dan felt the water flow off him, so by the time he reached Rack's unmade bed, he was dry.

Rack put him on the bed. "Have you ever slept with a man?"

"Do my cousins count?"

Rack laughed. "Not unless you slept naked with them."

Dan smiled, "Then, no."

Rack brought his hand down to Dan's member, smaller than Rack's, Dan noticed.

"You're missing something."

"They ... they cut it off when I'm a teenager. It means I'm a man."

"How horrible," said Rack, stroking him. "But I can see it works fine."

Dan began to pant, thrusting his hips forward into Rack's hand.

"That feels so good when you do that."

"This will feel better," Rack said, and bent his head.

He licked Dan's chest and nipples. Dan arched his back as Rack saturated the nipple with his saliva, then his other hand's fingers rubbed around the wet nipple, while his head bent to the other nipple.

The sensations were so intense, Dan didn't know where to turn, where to thrust, what to hold onto. He ended up gripping the sheets, thrusting his hips up. He cried out, thrusting forward, and exploded in Rack's hand.

Rack held onto him as he spent himself. Dan and collapsed on the bed while Rack continued to milk his member, drawing out every last drop.

Dan fell asleep, feeling Rack's tongue on his abdomen, licking up the sticky fluid.

3

The cock's crow found them with Rack curled around a sleeping Dan.

Rack stroked Dan's chest and pulled him slowly out of sleep. "I have to get up."

"Sun's up already?"

"Uh huh." Dan huddled in the covers. Rack chuckled. "Sleep in, city boy. I'll go get the eggs."

Dan yawned. "Do we have a lot to do today?"

"Wash day," he said. "It's going to rain tonight." He looked at Dan. "Want to milk the cows?"

"I ... uh, don't know how."

"Or wash clothes."

"I'll wash clothes." He'd seen his mother do it. How hard was it?

He found out how hard, using a washboard and the tub and a short stool intended for that purpose. He skinned his knuckles too many times and had a new respect for his mother. There wasn't even a wringer in the bathroom that he could use, so he had to do it by hand.

To wash two pairs of dungarees and four shirts, along with underwear and socks took him until lunch. After lunch, he hung the laundry outside while Rack fixed some things around the house and barn. Dan's arms were tired and his hands were red by the time he finally sat down to rest, sometime around three o'clock.

Rack came in with the clothes a short time after Dan hung them out.

"They're dry already?"

"Yes, and thank you for doing that for me."

"I don't know if I want to do it again."

Rack laughed. "It takes me half the time, but I cheat." He folded the clothes and brought them upstairs, leaving Dan's clothes on the couch. "Ready to go to the dance?"

"It's on the reservation?"

"Yes. We'll have to take the truck because I don't have an extra saddle."

They rode out to Military Road and then followed a road next to the railroad tracks.

Dan asked, "What did that Indian call you?"

"*Kmowin?*" He chuckled. "You'll see."

They came upon a spot where horses and wagons were pulled together in a large clearing. Seated in a large circle people watched as the men set up the bonfire. People were spread out on blankets on the grass, which was dry and mowed down like Rack's fields. Rack and Dan sat down on the prickly grass.

"It's going to be a while," Rack said. "They have to wait until sunset."

In the meantime, many Indians came to Rack, introduced themselves to Dan. Some spoke only the Indian language, which Rack understood and spoke perfectly, while others spoke English. They kept calling him *Kmowin*, and seemed genuinely happy to see him.

Dan said, "I thought people didn't like you."

"Most people in town don't. But these people respect me."

The crowd started getting bigger, and, by sunset, the circle was two rows deep and looked about 200 yards wide. Someone in Indian buckskin came to the bonfire and lit it. When he did, everyone said a phrase.

"They all said, 'We are Keepers of the Fire'," said Rack. "They begin the dance now."

Women came out, dressed in Indian costume, and started dancing around the fire. There was drumming and shaking of rattles that seemed to go deep into the ground. There were no words, just the drum beat. Dan felt it go into his bones, rattle inside, hit some primal part of his brain.

What would his father think of him now?

The women finished their dance, and then men came out in costume, in feathers and fringe. There was singing and drumming.

"That is Eagle," said Rack.

Dan watched the man twist and move, turn around and dance freely, while another man danced behind him, hunched over.

"Prairie Dog."

The man would bob his head up and then down, like a prairie dog did in the wild.

More animals came out. Rabbit. Dog. Last came Crow.

"He carries the storm clouds," Rack said.

Rack turned his face to the sky and closed his eyes. He put his hands on the grass, fingers digging into the earth. He seemed to be in a trance, caught up in the drumming. Dan looked around, but no one was watching them.

Dan heard a rumble in the distance. The Crow halted his dance, freezing in place, and people went silent. Over the crackle of the fire, he heard it again. He saw a flash of lightning in the sky, far away.

Crow set himself down on two legs and cawed. The dancing and singing started again in earnest, like a celebration, and he went around the fire one more time.

"It's going to rain," said Rack in a strange, distant voice. His head came down, eyes still closed. "For two days. The Earth is thirsty."

Dan stared at Rack, who then opened his eyes. He took a deep breath, letting it out slowly. How did Rack know? The dancing stopped, and a man came out, again in Indian dress, and threw something onto the fire. It sparked, and Dan smelled the scent of it on the air: tobacco.

Dan felt a drop on his hand. Then another.

Everyone started to get up.

"Time to go," Rack said. "It'll be raining by the time we leave."

The rumble got louder, as the lights in the sky shot through the clouds. People saw Rack, muttering "*Iwgwien*," as they went by.

"What are they saying?" Dan asked him.

"Thank you."

"For what?"

Rack held out his hand, letting drops fall onto his palm. "For this." He looked up at the sky.

At that moment, the skies broke open and the rain came down in force. Dan ducked his head and ran back to the truck. People ran in all directions trying to get out of the rain. Rack just walked in it, without a care in the world.

Finally, Rack climbed into the truck and joined the traffic out of the clearing, then turned left on the road, leaving the reservation. The rain was coming down in buckets.

"How can you see in this?" Dan asked.

The rain came down in a river while the windshield wipers tried their best to clear the rivulets.

"The water is my element, my friend," Rack said.

Now it came to Dan. "*You* made it rain."

"Yes, I did."

"That's your Indian name. Rainmaker."

"He-Who-Makes-Rain but yes, the same thing."

"How can you do that?"

"It's a long story."

"Tell me."

He said, "I'll tell you when I get back home. Let me concentrate."

Dan fell silent as the headlights pierced through the darkness, illuminating just a short distance before them. They slowed down at a fence, and then turned up a driveway. Dan had no idea if it was their driveway or not.

The truck pulled up to the house, gray in the dark, and Rack said, "All right, let's go."

He dove out of the truck, in the middle of the storm, while Dan hesitated. He was closer to the porch, closer to the edge, but he would still get wet. He took a deep breath and ran out of the truck, slamming the door shut, and joined Rack on the porch.

Rack put his arm around Dan and led him into the house. Both men were soaked through, even in the short distance it took from the truck to the porch.

"How?" asked Dan.

"How what?"

"How did you do it?"

Rack smiled. "A very long time ago, I lived among what the Latins called the *Lutici*. We called ourselves

Luczh. I died of a wasting disease and went to the underworld." He paused, to let that sink in.

Dan said, "You died?"

"Yes."

"But you're alive."

"I came back."

"How?"

"A goddess came and brought me back. I've come to help people. I bring them rain and water. It's part of my power."

Dan leaned his head into Rack's shoulder and uttered a small sigh. "I think I love you," he said.

"You think," Rack chuckled. "You're how old?"

"Twenty-two."

"I thought you were older."

"If you lived with the Romans, then that was at least … almost 1900 years ago."

"The *Latins*. I died in 926. So about a thousand years."

"You've lived for a thousand years?" Dan gazed up at Rack.

Rack turned into the path to his house. "You don't seem that concerned. You're more worried that I'm alone." He smiled down at Dan. "That's very kind of you."

Dan hit Rack's hard body with his hand. "Stop doing that!"

Rack laughed, as the punch didn't even hurt. "I'm sorry, I can't help it."

"That's why nobody likes you — you know what they're thinking."

"Not what they're thinking, what they're feeling." He hugged Dan to him as he pulled into the barn. "Go into the house. I'll be there shortly."

"Rack?"

"Hm?"

Dan turned, took Rack's soaking wet head in both of his hands, and kissed his wet lips. Rack grunted in surprise, but didn't pull away. He cupped the back of Dan's head and pulled him in further. Their tongues slid along each other's, and both men moaned, giving in. Rack put his other arm around Dan, while Dan wrapped his arms around Rack.

Dan said, "I'm going to help you and then I want to do more than just kiss you."

"Then the sooner we get in the house, the sooner you can do that."

Rack opened the door and let him inside.

In the dark, Dan grabbed Rack by the front of his shirt and kissed him madly.

"You're soaking wet," he said, starting to unbutton Rack's shirt.

"I can take care of that," he said, and Dan felt the shirt get dry under his fingers. Water flowed onto the floor, into a puddle.

"Amazing," whispered Dan. Rack stepped out of the puddle to the bottom step. Dan reached for him, and Rack took his hand, drawing him upstairs.

4

"It's Sunday," Rack said two days later, throwing open the curtains to the bedroom. Wan sunlight streamed in.

Dan realized this was the first time he had not kept the Sabbath — unless being in bed almost all day making love to someone he professed it to counted.

"I have to go to church," Rack said, disgusted.

"Why?"

"To see and be seen. If I don't go to church every once in a while, then they think I'm holding pagan rites out here and will come up my road and threaten me." He smiled at Dan. "Not to say that I'm not holding pagan rites." He kissed Dan over the bed. "Wear your Sunday best if you have it."

Dan got his bag and emptied it out in the living room. There was an extra *yarmluke* and his *tallit* in the bag. He threw those aside in disgust.

Rack came into the living room just in time to see those items.

"Ah," he said, and picked up the shawl. "Now I see. Tomorrow, you can send a post to your family. They'll be worried."

"Father will disown me." Dan looked at the *tallit*. "Mother will mourn."

"A family is important, Dan. Sometimes, that's all you have."

"I don't want to marry that woman."

"Tell them you don't want to marry at all."

"But my father wants to continue the family name."

"You can do what most people do - marry her and live away from her. Father her children and be done with it."

"That's even worse. I would abandon her."

"Or find a woman that you like and —" Rack stopped, seeing Dan's face. "I see." Rack smiled.

"See what?"

"You told me not to tell you what you're feeling."

"You'll do it anyway."

Rack laughed, placed his hand on Dan's shoulder. "That's right. You don't want to love anyone else right now."

"Ever," he said, looking up at Rack's eyes.

"You'd better get dressed, or I'll change my mind about going to town."

They both rode into St. Mary's. Dan had never been to a gentile service, so Rack would have to explain what to do.

The rain had ushered in Fall, so the air was cooler than it had been in days. Rack parked his wagon far from the others, paid a man to watch it, and they started down the street to the church.

Rack stood apart from the crowd of people near the church, but Dan could tell that they were looking at him with hooded eyes. Young women watched him, tiny smiles playing on their faces, and Rack tipped his hat to them. Some giggled. Dan got a fire in his chest, walking closer to Rack whenever he came upon women.

Then came the older, more matronly women, who looked down their noses at Rack. Dan couldn't understand why. Last came the men, gathered in small groups talking, waiting for the bell to the church to ring.

"Excuse me," he said to Dan, "I need to talk to someone. Can you wait right here?"

Dan nodded, and stood alone between the matrons and the gentlemen. An older woman was staring at him, and finally broke from the women she was with and came over to him.

"Hello, young man. You're new to the Mission?"

"Yes, ma'am," he said, and took her hand lightly, thumb on the top of her hand.

"Oh, a gentleman, too!" She looked over at her ladies and nodded, then turned to him, smiling. "What's a young man like you doing with a thief like Mr. Morse?"

In the time he had known Rack, he'd never asked his full name. "Thief, ma'am?"

"I'm sure he wouldn't have told you. Come over here, young man. What's your name?"

"Dan. Dan Gold."

"Mr. Gold, yes. I am Mrs. Brock, and this is Mrs. Palmer …" He was introduced to four women, who offered their hands and he bowed over them.

"Please, Mrs. Somerset, tell Mr. Gold about Mr. Morse."

"Oh, that *man*," said Mrs. Somerset, rolling her eyes. "He swindled my husband out of thirty acres of land."

"How did he do that?"

"Well!" She leaned over. "You see, he started farming on that land, and when my husband tried to put a fence, he took it down, saying it was his! Then my husband had to pay for a surveyor, and then *he* paid for a surveyor, and because *he* paid more money, the surveyor ruled in his favor!"

Said Mrs. Brock, "No one works on his farm."

The fourth woman, Mrs. Harvey, had said nothing to this point. The other women looked to Mrs. Harvey, and so did Dan. Her eyes were watery, but her countenance was angry.

"He," she said slowly through gritted teeth, "took away everything."

"She lost her farm. She lost everything," said Mrs. Brock.

"He talked my husband into signing a will," she said, still angry. "Leaving him everything, and he died a month later."

Mrs. Harvey wiped angry tears and glared beyond Dan. Dan turned around to see Rack standing alone, waiting.

The church bell rang.

Mrs. Brock put a comforting hand on Dan's arm. "Please, young man, get out while you can."

A man took Mrs. Brock's arm and nodded to Dan, then escorted her into the church. Rack, his hands in his pockets, went up to Dan. "Let me guess."

"Did you?"

"Did I what?"

He nodded toward the women. "Do what they say you did?"

"What did they say I did?"

"You swindled them out of some land?"

Rack shrugged. "I probably did."

"You took one woman's house."

"Oh, Harvey? He owed me money from gambling debts on the race horses. He said he'd just sign his farm over to me. I took it."

"And his widow? And orphan?"

"Pshaw, she's got money from a pension. Besides," he snorted. "She tried to chase me."

"She did?"

"One thing you'll learn about this town is that everyone here has some story about me that's bad. I've done nothing but good for these people. I've kept the land. I've lived my life. I help where I can. But it's not good enough for them. They're money-greedy, land-grabbing snakes who don't know how to love the Earth and take care of their own families. They're out for themselves."

"So you play their game, too?"

Rack's eyes flashed in anger.

They approached the door to the church. The priest noticed the two of them.

"Mr. Morse," he said. "It's good to see you again."

"Good to see you too, Father Guillet. This is Dan. It's his first mass here."

"Hello, Dan. I hope you'll be staying in town."

"That remains to be seen," he said, looking at Rack.

Rack sat in one of the pews that had room. Dan noted the service was long. Dan couldn't talk to Rack in the church.

After the service, they went outside. They started down the street when someone called, "Excuse me, Mr. Gold!"

Dan turned around to see a man walking briskly in their direction. Dan stopped and waited for the man to catch up.

"Ah, Mr. Gold. I'm Mr. Robert Brock. My wife was talking to you earlier."

"Yes, Mr. Brock." Dan shook his hand.

Brock was pointedly ignoring Rack, who waited beside Dan.

"We were wondering if you would like to join us for Sunday dinner today."

"If Rack doesn't mind." Dan looked at Rack.

Said Rack coldly, "He's asking you, not me."

Dan looked to Brock, then back to Rack. "Do you mind?"

"Of course not. Have a good time." Rack kept walking down the street to his wagon.

"I'm so glad you decided to come," said Mrs. Brock when Mr. Brock brought Dan to their carriage.

It was a nice covered carriage, something he was used to, pulled by two mares. They had a Negro driver, who opened the door for them to get in. Dan sat next to Mr. Brock, as was expected of a man of his station.

"It's so seldom we have guests," she said, and prattled on about the town, about buildings that were built with funds provided by them, buildings named after them, streets named after them. The Brocks let it be known that in this town, they were rich ones. Dan's father always said it was good to cultivate the rich gentiles - one never knew when they would be useful.

They went through a gated area with a tall wrought-iron fence surrounding it. The carriage went down a long lane, heading to a large box-shaped house with colonnades. He got out of the carriage, staring up at it in awe.

Mrs. Brock offered her hand to Dan, who took it, and escorted her to the building. He had seen houses like this in New York, but on a much smaller scale. Everything was so big here. A servant took his jacket and offered him cold lemonade. They walked through the house, Mrs. Brock showing him all her artwork and awards she had gotten from the town. They went to the dining room and were served a three-course luncheon.

Dan noticed all they talked about were themselves. When Mr. Brock asked Dan where he was from, Mr. Brock went into a long diatribe about his brother in New York City, how they lived much better here in the country, and did Dan know that Brock was applying to be a member on the board of directors for the bank they were planning to develop in town?

They didn't care about Dan. They talked and talked about nothing in particular, nothing of import to him. They didn't talk about their farm, the land — only when it meant the amount of money it was making them.

Dan missed Rack. Finally, he said, "I'm sorry, I'm very fatigued."

Both of them looked worried. "You must rest, then," said Mr. Brock, getting up from the table.

"I need to go home — back to the farm."

"Are you sure you want to go there?"

"All of my things are there. I would love to stay here, but ..."

"Of course, of course." Brock snapped his fingers, and the butler came running. "See to it that Mr. Gold is safely returned to the Morse farm."

"Yes, sir," said the butler, bowing. "Right this way, sir."

"Thank you for a lovely luncheon," said Dan, taking Mrs. Brock's hand and shaking Mr. Brock's.

"Please come back again!" called Mrs. Brock.

Not if I can help it, he thought, and followed the butler to the door. Getting his hat and coat, Dan climbed into the carriage. He leaned back into the carriage with a sigh.

Finally, quiet. He wanted Rack. He wanted his simple life. Well, maybe hire someone to do the washing. The carriage stopped. Dan leaned out the window to see what was going on. It looked like some cowboys were ... robbing the bank?

"What's —"

His carriage door opened. A man in a beaten and weathered cowboy hat with one white eye and one blue one leered at him.

"Lookit we got here!"

The man reached in to grab Dan, but Dan kicked him in the face and slammed shut the door, holding the handle tight.

"Gah, you scrawny little shit!"

The man outside tried the handle but Dan held it fast. Those few days on the farm improved his strength. He heard a snap, and then someone stuck their hands in the windows which had no glass, only curtains. Dan ducked out of the way of them, still holding onto the door handle.

"What's in there?"

"Who the hell cares? Tip it over!"

Dan looked around wildly, as they started to rock the carriage.

"Heave!" he heard a bunch of men yell.

The carriage tipped onto the side without a door. Dan tumbled against it, landing hard against the windows, snapping their fragile frames. He shook his head, slightly dazed, and shoved off the cushions that had fallen off the seats. Dan saw someone tear off the door and look inside.

"It's a man," said a big man, leaning into the carriage.

Dan tried to make himself small, getting out of the way of someone's grasping hands, but they grabbed a hold of his hair and pulled. Dan yelled as they pulled him out of the broken doorway and flopped him onto the street, in the dirt. Someone put one foot on his back.

"Lookit what we have here," said someone, as another person lifted his head by the hair. He stared into a man's bloody face. "You broke my nose, you runt."

The man hauled off and hit Dan right in the face. Dan rolled with it, tipping over onto his back. The man kicked him in the ribs, and Dan grunted. He struggled to get up, but the man took him by the hair again and lifted him from the ground, yanking him to his feet. He stumbled and the man twirled him around. The man hit him again in the ribs, then threw him back into the dirt, face down.

Dan brought his hands up near his face, to try and push himself up. The man grabbed him by the hair again. This time he wound up, getting ready to hit.

"*Put him down!*"

Dan almost swooned at that voice. "Oh, thank God," he muttered.

The man dropped Dan with a thud. "Who the hell are you?"

Dan again brought his hands up to his shoulders and pushed himself up to his knees.

"What are you doing to my town?" Rack demanded.

"Your town. *Your* town?" The man laughed.

Dan saw it coming. "Rack, look out!"

Two men came at Rack from opposite sides of the street. Rack kept walking, oblivious to them.

The two men grabbed a hold of him. Rack stopped walking. He glared at the man.

"Whatcha gonna do now, big man?"

Rack hunched over, his eyes full of fury. The men on either side of him started to bleed from their ears, then their eyes. They slid off him, sinking to the ground, gurgling, then wheezing, and then they were still.

"Leave," said Rack, again in that strange voice he had the night with the Indians.

"You think a trick will sc—" He put his hand to his throat. "scare—". It came out as a wheeze, then a whisper. He tried to cough, but it came out as a soundless hack. The man started to bleed just like the other ones. Dan watched the man fall, his hand reaching toward Rack.

"You hurt my family," Rack said angrily, and watched the man die at his feet.

Dan looked up at Rack, then back at the body, then up at Rack. People moved away from the scene. Rack stepped over the man's body and approached Dan.

He put his hand on Dan's cheek. "Are you all right?" he asked.

Dan burst into tears.

5

The townsfolk avoided Dan like they avoided Rack. No one would speak to him. When he went to send a postcard to his family, the postmaster was short and curt with him.

Within a month, Dan lost most of his city-boy look and started to get muscles he never had before. The soreness eventually went away, as Rack massaged those muscles in the bath that was always warm.

They went to town one afternoon and saw from a playbill that a carnival had arrived just outside of town. Dan had never seen a country carnival. With Dan acting like an excited schoolboy, Rack could hardly say no.

As they were in town, the carnival put on a parade. There was a lion in a cage, some prancing clowns, and a pair of women on a horse. On another horse stood a Robin Hood with a bow and arrow.

Rack stood with Dan, in the front row. He said, "I know him."

"Who?" asked Dan.

Then Robin Hood notched an arrow and fired it into the air. People scattered, not knowing where it would land.

It landed precisely at Rack's feet.

"Him," said Rack, pulling the arrow out of the ground.

He touched its tip to his forehead to salute Robin. Robin touched the brim of his peaked cap as he continued down the street with the horse. Following him were some tumblers, and a wagon of women, waving their handkerchiefs at men. Some dropped their hanky while other men picked them up.

"Do you think we can meet him?"

"I *know* that we can meet him," said Rack. He shook the arrow. "I have to give this back to him, don't I?"

A clown came around passing a hat, and Rack put a coin in it.

"Thank you, sir, may God bless you!"

Rack nodded. "Let's follow the parade."

They got the wagon and followed the dust the parade made back to the carnival grounds. It was just a bit south of town, on the banks of the Kansas River. Rack brought the wagon to the outskirts and the two men jumped off. Three men walked in their direction.

One was a very large bald man with a big mustache — a Russian by his looks. Another was a man of medium height with a hook for a hand. The last was man of normal height, but he had the attitude of a leader.

"We're not open," said the leader.

Rack looked at the three men. "Seems that Robin Hood gave me this." He held up the arrow.

The man reached for it. "I'll see that he gets it."

"I'd rather give it to him personally."

"What is going on, gentlemen?" said a woman with a silky Russian accent. Dan saw a petite woman with long, luxurious black hair and dark eyes, dressed in a flowing black dress. She studied Rack and said, "Ah, you are expected." She beckoned.

Rack glanced at the three men, and he followed her. Dan jumped a bit and followed them both.

They walked through the carnival. It was still setting up some areas. Three huge tents were up. A few different types of wagons gathered around the tents. One had a fortune teller on it. Another had the women in it. Dan saw Rack kept his eyes ahead, so he did the same thing.

They came to a small tent. The woman pushed back the flap and said to the person inside, "You owe me two bits."

"For what?" said a man.

"Please go in." She bowed and waved her hand to show them inside.

Dan and Rack stepped into the tent. It took a minute for his eyes to adjust to the wan ight.

A white man with reddish-brown hair stood there, half-undressed. He wore only underwear and was pulling off a pair of tights. He was big and broad like Rack, but his muscles were all in his chest and shoulders.

He finished getting the tights off and said, "Cancer, it *is* you!"

"Saj," Rack said, and pulled the man into a hug.

Dan felt that fire in his chest again, what he realized was jealousy.

Rack put his arm around Saj's shoulders and said, "This is Dan."

With a smile, Saj shook Dan's hand. "I see that we're going to lose you, Rak. *Su'e-zeh.*"

"*Sud Ishtar,*" Rack said. He turned to Dan. "This is my brother, Sagittarius."

"Saj for short," he said. "Though here I'm Robin Hood. Or David Archer."

Dan said, looking between the two, "You don't look like brothers."

Rack turned to Dan. "Remember when I told you that I died and came back?"

"He did too?" asked Dan, surprised.

"Yep," Saj said. Rack handed the arrow back to Saj. He looked at the arrow, lost in thought for a moment, and then perked his head up with a smile. "Hey, I can get you two free tickets to the carnival tonight. Want to come? My treat."

"Sure, we'd love to."

"One condition, though."

"What's that?"

"I've got to work you into my act." His eyes twinkled. "It's a trick I've wanted to try but nobody wants to do it."

"Try?"

"I know I can do it. Just trust me."

Dan said, "My father always said to never trust a man who says, 'Trust me.'"

Rack said, smiling at Dan, "Your father was a brilliant man." He looked at Saj. "But I'll do it anyway."

"You'll love it. So will the crowd. And maybe they'll trust me to do it sometime!"

"What does it involve?"

"You standing still."

Rack shrugged. "All right."

"Good, I'll pick you out of the crowd tonight. Try and get a front row seat."

6

They ate in the tavern, and, when sundown came, they rode back to the carnival. With the two tokens that Saj gave them, they got in for free. Hucksters tried to get them involved in games, which Dan refused to participate in. Rack wasn't a gambler, either, so he just watched.

He put a hand on Dan's shoulder and they went to the big tent. It was starting to fill up, and kids took most of the first rows. Rack and Dan sat in the second row instead.

Rack pointed up, and Dan could see a trapeze set up in the rafters. Dan saw members from church come in with their children. Some passed by him without even a glance. A couple of the townsfolk did sit next to Dan. A woman holding a baby smiled at Dan. The man with her leaned forward and tipped his hat to Rack - Dan noticed it was one of the workers from the first day he worked on the farm.

Most of the people sitting in the tent were whites, though Dan saw a collection of Negros standing in the back or on the sides. Dan leaned over, "Why don't you hire a Negro to do the washing?"

Rack laughed, "Oh, don't like doing that anymore, do you? Then you can milk the cows or take care of the animals while I do the washing."

"Well, you can do it faster than me."

"Because I cheat," he said, leaning over to whisper in Dan's ear, and then giving it a quick lick. Dan sat up straight, and Rack chuckled lowly, patting Dan on the back.

A man came out to the middle of the ring. "Ladies and gentlemen! Welcome to the Derry Brothers Show! I am your host, Master Derry the elder! First, ladies and gentlemen, we bring out — the parade!"

A small horse-drawn flat cart came out carrying the clowns, who were playing instruments as they went around, followed by another flat wagon with men and women in tight clothes glittering in the lantern-light. They waved to the people as they went by. Along with them was Robin Hood, who bowed to women and waved. Following up at the end was the lion in the cage, and then, something they hadn't seen — an elephant. The entire room gasped as it came into the room. Dan stared, his eyes as wide as saucers.

"Have you ever seen one of those before?" Dan asked Rack.

"A long time ago, yes," he said quietly.

The elephant remained. A tall, thin man did also. Master Derry introduced the "180-year-old pachyderm" as "Louis," and the trainer as "Monsieur DeBourey". He had the elephant sit on a stool, legs up. Somewhere a cymbal crashed, and some people clapped. The audience got the hint and whenever the animal did something, a cymbal would sound, and people cheered.

"She's a very smart animal," said Rack, watching the elephant twirl in place.

"It's a she?"

"No tusks."

Then the elephant turned from them and, with her trunk, pulled a net out to the middle of the area. Master Derry came out and pointed upward, so everyone had to look up.

Above them were three trapeze artists, a man and a woman. They swung on what looked to Dan like rickety sticks attached by rope, twisting in the air catching each other. Then they took the net away and they did some more dangerous stunts. Dan couldn't watch; he was afraid to see them fall.

After the trapeze came the clowns, midgets all, about five of them. They tumbled and juggled while something else was being set up. When they got out of the ring, there was a large black curtain was in place.

Master Derry introduced "Cosmo the Magnificent", who appeared before them in a flash of smoke. Dan ribbed Rack — it was Saj.

He pulled rabbits out of hats. He made doves fly out of a handkerchief (the doves sat on his shoulder for the rest of the show), he pulled pennies out of children's ears. He swallowed fiery swords — he did a lot of things with fire.

Next came some tumblers, who cleared the place, then a pair of horsemen who jumped from horse to horse, or used the horse to do gymnastics. The horses galloped dangerously, or pranced around, with gymnasts performing feats of balance and poise.

Then came Robin Hood, who needed no introduction. Rack and Dan sat up straight. A pole was set up in the middle of the ring. Clowns came out dressed in black, like bad guys, and Robin shot at them while he galloped around the ring. They would fall, dying dramatically and humorously.

Robin switched arrows, while the clowns got up and ran to the back of the tent, to the applause of the people.

"I need a volunteer!"

All the kids in the front row raised their hands, and Robin looked down at them, smiling. He looked to the back; adults, women and men, many had their hands raised. Robin finally centered on Rack, and pointed to him.

Rack stepped down, and most of the townsfolk sighed in disappointment. Rack came down the few steps and stood before Robin.

"Sir, if you would please step to that pole over there."

Dan watched as Rack walked over to the pole. Then Robin took out an apple, shined it against his clothes, and showed it to the people. He put the apple on Rack's head. Rack said something, but nobody heard. Robin patted Rack's shoulder, then got back on the horse. He pulled out his bow and an arrow, then jumped onto the back of the horse so he was standing on its back.

Dan was at the edge of his seat, watching. Robin galloped the horse faster and faster around the ring; the entire room was hushed. Dan heard the arrow let loose, the *twang* of the bow, and he saw the arrow stick out of the apple, spearing it to the pole.

Cymbals crashed, and Dan breathed.

Then Rack crumpled to the ground.

"No!" Dan ran from his seat. At the same time Robin jumped off the horse and dashed to Rack. A couple of other people from the carnival came out of the wings too. Dan shoved by them staring at Rack. He had gone pasty white.

"He fainted," pronounced one of the tumblers.

The Master took out a flask, and passed it under Rack's nose.

The clown said, "You carry that thing around everywhere, don't you?"

Rack sniffed, coughed.

"It's useful," said the Master, and stood up. "He's all right, ladies and gentlemen!"

Robin, the tumblers, and Dan helped Rack to his feet. Rack slowly got his color back. Dan started to lead him back to their seats, but Rack said, "No, I need air."

They went outside, Rack leaning hard on Dan, taking in gasping lungfuls of air.

"Never doing that again," he said. "It was like staring down a barrel of a gun pointed right at you."

They wandered the midway a little bit, catching their bearings and breath. They stopped in front of the fortune teller's booth. She had no customers, but saw them and waved them over.

"I will read your fortunes for one bit."

Rack took out two coins and dropped them on the table. "Make it good."

"I tell the truth," she said, and shuffled the deck of cards. Rack held the chair out for Dan, who sat down.

She laid out the cards, looked at them for a moment, then up at the two of them and smiled. "You are lovers, and this is good."

Dan's face went red.

"You will receive a message, and a visit," she said, looking at Dan. "Both are not wanted." She then turned to Rack. "You must defend him. His past comes to haunt both of you."

She looked among the cards again and then said, "The crab will succeed, so long as he is by the river. Leave the land to those who can take care of it. This is the last time the crab is by the river."

Rack exhaled sharply. "Good," he said.

Dan looked up at Rack. "What does that mean?"

"It means I can't leave where I am." He bent his head to the cards. "What does this one mean?" He pointed to a card with four cups.

She smiled, and looked up at them. "You are joined in the heavens, and by the sight of God."

Rack put a hand on Dan's shoulder, and rested his chin on Dan's head. He nuzzled Dan's hair. Dan stiffened, everywhere, but Rack didn't seem to care.

The woman laughed. "Also, you will gain more land, if you give."

"That's my plan," he said, straightening. "Any more?"

"You will both need to fight for what you want — and what you want is each other."

Rack removed his hand from Dan's shoulder. Dan coughed.

"Thank you," Dan said, trying to fight the blush.

"You are welcome!" she said, gathering her cards. "*Devlesa!*"

"*Devlesa*," said Rack, as Dan got up. When he turned to go, he saw Saj standing a few feet away.

"I didn't want to disturb you," Saj said.

He wore plain clothes, hand his hands deep in his pockets. He looked embarrassed. His hands clenched into fists, Dan stalked over to Saj, and socked him in the mouth.

"That's for almost killing him!"

Saj took the punch, and felt the side of his mouth. "I deserved that, I guess."

"You could have told me what you were going to do," said Rack.

"I did. I told you to stand still."

"Very funny."

"I knew what I was doing! I've been shooting since before you were born! Well, not you, Rak, but *you!*" He pointed to Dan.

"And what's with the magic?"

"If I have the power, I might as well use it. Besides, a lot of it is Chinese fireworks."

"You're going to draw attention to yourself."

"As if we don't already, with our choice of partners."

"Now we do. In the old days, that wasn't true."

"In *your* old days. In my old days, it was a scandal. Or would have been if we got caught."

"Which is why we don't get caught, do we?"

Saj shrugged, stuck his hands in his pockets again.

"Be careful."

"Why? Nobody's out to get us."

"Yes, there is," said Dan.

"What?"

"Hubris."

Rack laughed. "Out of the mouths of babes," he said, and put an arm around Dan's shoulder. "We have to get home." They started walking away.

"Say," called Saj, "Can I interest you in doing that trick again tomorrow night?"

7

The next morning, Dan was awakened by a kiss. "I have to go into town," said Rack. "I'm taking the wagon."

"Ahum," Dan murmured, and turned over.

Rack kissed Dan again on the top of his head and left.

When Dan finally got out of bed, it was full morning, and the sunlight was streaming into the windows of the house. He got up, stretched, and yawned. Rack hadn't come back yet. That was unusual.

He went downstairs, calling for him, but there was no answer. He went out among the animals, but he wasn't there, either. He was heading back to the house when a man on a horse came riding up the lane. He wasn't in a hurry, but he did seem to have purpose.

"Are you Jordan Goldblum?"

Dan looked around, "Uh, yes."

"Letter for you." He handed it to him.

Dan could tell by the script before he saw the address. The horseman waited.

"Thank you," Dan said, looking down at the letter.

The man snorted and pulled the horse away from Dan, then trotted back to the road. Dan went into the house and used a knife to tear open the letter.

When Rack arrived home, Dan was sitting on the bench outside of the house. Rack saw the sad look on Dan's face. He jumped down from the wagon, pulling the horse toward the stairs. "What's wrong?"

"My parents." He thrust out a piece of paper.

"Is something wrong?" Rack walked up the steps and took the paper, reading it.

"They want me to go to Boston and leave here. They said the Mendelsons are really angry."

Rack read through the letter, his eyes squinting. "Who's Harold?"

"My sister's husband."

Rack laughed, "They actually will send him here to get you if you don't go back?" Rack handed the letter back. "Over my dead body."

Dan looked relieved.

"You should know me better than that," Rack said. "Come help me with the horses."

Dan followed Rack into the barn, and as they took the horse off the wagon, Dan started talking. "Harold gets what he wants, Rack."

"So do I, if it's as important as you are."

"Don't kill him."

Rack said quietly, "I only kill if it's a last resort."

He sighed and thought fleetingly of the men who had bled to death in the dusty street a few short months ago.

As they sat watching the sunset, Rack tousled Dan's hair and whispered, "Everything will be all right."

8

The next morning, just after cock's crow, Dan saw another man come up the lane. Dan was outside letting the cows out, and Rack went out to meet him. Dan finished what he was doing and joined Rack.

It was Saj. Rack was holding some tickets in his hand while talking to Saj. He waved to Dan.

"Hello, sorry we parted on such bad terms. What can I do to make it up to you?"

"Not do that again," Dan said.

Saj laughed. "Don't worry. Nobody wants to touch that trick with a ten-foot pole." He looked at Rack, "And I'm sorry for making you the town laughing-stock."

"It won't last long. I'll get my reputation back in a few months. Widow Moore is failing fast."

"Pasture?"

"Alfalfa, better house than this. East of me, right across the road."

"Oh, that reminds me." He tucked a hand in his pocket and took out a square piece of metal about the size of a dollar with etchings on them. "For luck."

Rack nodded, taking the metal. "Happy travels, Sagittarius."

"Happy living, Cancer. Good luck, the two of you." He nodded to them both, then left.

Dan inclined his head toward the tickets. "What are those for?"

"For next time they come through." Rack went back to the barn. "I gave them a donation of some hay."

"Even after that bastard almost killed you?"

"They're a family," Rack said. "Like we're a family."

9

Dan never sent a letter back to his parents, as if daring them to send Harold. Christmas came, and Rack put up a tree. Dan didn't bother with a menorah, but liked the gentile Christmas better, with the tree and presents, and their legends of Santa Claus.

Winter gave way to spring. Widow Moore had, in fact, died over the winter and by some stroke of luck or the way the will was written, her son got her land. Her son was in Texas, doing fine ranching down there, so Rack made him an offer. The son took it, and Rack added 105 acres to his sprawling farm of 400 or so acres. He was connected to Soldier's Creek and extended his northern border to be along the reservation.

One day in April, they went to the town to get some supplies. Dan got bigger and sprouted a beard. Rack gave him an old beat-up jacket that was still a bit big on him. Dan didn't fit in any of his clothes from New York anymore.

He went to the general store with Rack. The owner of the store was one of the few people who didn't treat Rack like he was less than human, and he was fighting off the constant attempts of the bankers to put him out of business. He sold to anyone - black, white, Indian - the same prices, the same things. Most of the upper class did not even come near the general store, preferring to go to Wichita for their items.

Rack was busy packing some things into the wagon while Dan went into the store, looking around at the candy. He wanted to get something sweet for Rack, and didn't want Rack to know.

Dan picked out some rock candy and pocketed it after giving the owner a couple of pennies for it. The owner smiled, knowing who they were for.

"Oh, by the way, someone came here looking for you the other week."

"For me?"

The owner nodded. "Described you, except now you have a beard, and you don't have those funny hats."

"Funny hat?"

"He had one too. A black hat. Sat on the back of his head. Long hair, too. Was surprised he wasn't run out of town."

Dan went white. "The other week? How long ago?"

"Oh, I reckon ... Mrs. Parker paid her bill that day, so ..." He glanced at the calendar. "Yes, two weeks this Friday." The owner said quietly, "Someone you owe money to?"

Dan blinked, "No. No, I mean, yes — mean — I owe him something." Dan leaned forward. "I was never here."

"Well, I didn't tell him you were, but I heard Brock told him."

Dan's eyes widened. "Oh. Oh, no." He ran out to find Rack, his worst fears realized.

Three men on horses were pointing rifles at Rack, who had his hands up. A fourth man in a suit stood watching Rack. His eyes - then his head - moved up to see Dan.

"Jordan," said the man. "Get over here."

He dismounted. The three men kept their guns on Rack while the man in the suit and the round Jewish hat stood next to his horse.

"I said come here."

Dan looked at Rack. Rack shook his head a little.

Dan stood defiantly and said, "No."

The fourth man waved his hand and all the men fired. Rack yelled and fell to the ground. With a cry of anguish, Dan ran to Rack's side. Rack was bleeding from wounds in his belly. He glared up at the two men with a look of pure rage and fury crossing his face.

Clouds seemed to appear out of nowhere, quick, thick and black, with thunder rolling in the distance. Dan held Rack, who was trying to push himself to a standing position while the man in the suit came over to them. "You're coming home with me now," the man said.

"No, I'm not, Harold. You can't make me!"

"Shoot him again," said the suit, grabbing at Dan's arm. Dan shrugged him off, still holding onto Rack, his arms around Rack's upper body.

Then the man stepped back. Rack got himself to a standing position while Dan stood in front of him, shielding him with his body.

"I don't believe it," said Harold. "I don't believe that you're with this … man."

Dan again stared defiantly. "You shoot him, you're going to have to go through me."

"No, Dan," rumbled Rack. "They can shoot me all they want, but I'll never die, not with you."

"How disgusting," sneered Harold and he looked at the three men with guns. "Kill them both."

"Ain't no killing happening near my store!" yelled the owner, standing out back holding a shotgun aimed at the three men on the horses.

"No, Thomas, no," said Rack, standing on his own two feet.

"Hands up," said a cool, calm voice.

Dan looked over the wagon to see the sheriff. The three men turned to Harold. "You said there weren't no sheriff in this town."

"Obviously," said the sheriff, "he was wrong. Hands up, boys."

"Shit," one said, throwing down his gun.

Harold went to the sheriff. "Tell me, Sheriff, how much would it take for you to turn right around and walk down that alley and pretend you didn't see anything?"

Rack was taking deep breaths as the sheriff narrowed his eyes at Harold.

"Bribery?" The sheriff waved his gun. "Come with me to the jail, and we can talk about this like sensible men."

"Sensible men, yes," said Harold with a grin, and then turned to the three men. "I'll be back gentlemen."

"Hell with this," said one of the men, turning his horse and nearly galloping away. The last man didn't move, looking back and forth between the retreating back of Harold and the man who rode away. Rack glared at him.

Then the hail came. Hail like bullets from the sky. The man ducked, but got pelted with hail. The one who dropped his gun took off, but was bleeding. Thomas ran into the store. Dan realized that neither Rack or himself were getting pelted by the hail.

The hail hit the horse and made it rear, throwing the remaining man to the ground. Rack ignored the man and walked around the wagon, heading to the street. People were running for cover, as the hail got bigger. Dan followed Rack as he headed toward the jail.

Windows broke as the hail hit them. Horses fell, injured. A ball-sized chunk of hail fell right in front of Dan. The sheriff ran across the street to the jailhouse, leaving Harold behind.

Harold stood in the middle of the street, getting pelted, not knowing where to turn. Rack kept walking, right up to him. He grabbed Harold by the front of his shirt and lifted him. A huge chunk of hail clocked Harold in the head, making him go limp.

"No one takes him away from me!" Rack yelled over the pounding of the hail. "Go back to New York or I'll kill you the next time I see you."

Then he threw the man a good ten feet away, sliding in the ice and hail, which now turned into a cold, miserable rainstorm that drenched everything, including Dan and Rack.

Dan reached Rack, who turned around to him, and put his arm around his shoulders.

"We're going home."

PISCES

MAY 2, 1862
NEW ORLEANS, LOUISIANA

I

D AVID LECROIX TAPPED THE QUILL AGAINST HIS CHIN as he looked at the dead body on the table. Its chest was exposed, cut open and its organs lay on the other table across from him. He dipped the quill in the inkwell and wrote:

"Heart, lungs unremarkable. Liver extensively distended, larger than normal."

He got up, washed his hands. It was something he had learned in France, something that most doctors here in the States thought was a worthless ritual. He pushed back his cowlick and turned to the body. The young man had been handsome, but his sudden collapse and death in the street caused some of the older, more superstitious to think he had the Plague.

LeCroix placed the organs back in the body. They would be removed by the undertaker anyway. He sewed up the chest as a man in a blue Union uniform walked in, holding a handkerchief to his face.

"So?" he asked, his voice muffled.

"Alcohol," said LeCroix.

The man removed the handkerchief. "Thank God."

LeCroix only shrugged. "You're going to bury him in the common graves?"

"We can't send him back to Pennsylvania," said the man. "The general will be happy to hear that it's not the plague."

"Tell the news reporters waiting outside. I have to get back to my patients." He washed his hands of the sticky blood.

"I'm not going to talk to them."

LeCroix sighed. "Jesus." He wiped his hands and tossed the towel on the body. "Sergeant, I'm not the one who spread the rumor that this man had the plague."

The sergeant glanced at the body, gulped, and looked up at LeCroix. "I can't."

"I'll do it. Jesus Christ."

He covered the body with a dirty, bloody sheet. "Contact the undertaker to get this body out of here. I don't want to see it when I come back down here."

"Yes, sir," said the sergeant automatically.

LeCroix pushed past the sergeant and went upstairs. He thought fleetingly of locking the sergeant down there, but then the body would never leave. He went up another set of stairs, heading into the hospital.

Since he was the head surgeon of the hospital, the news reporters waited for him in the lobby. In order for him to get into the hospital, he had to walk through that section. LeCroix sighed, putting his hand on the handle.

He hadn't even changed out of the bloody clothes. He opened the door.

Five reporters rushed at him. He had no idea who they were. They all looked him over, noticing the bloody white coat and pants.

"He doesn't have the plague," said LeCroix, before anyone said anything. "He died of rotgut."

"Did he have syphilis?" asked one of the reporters.

"No."

"He was last seen in the Main street brothel," said one of the other reporters. "Did that have anything to do with it?"

"I doubt it."

Four of them asked all the questions. The fifth one was in the back, taking down what everyone was saying. Finally, he asked, "What's rotgut?"

The other reporters laughed. LeCroix smiled at him. He looked like a chestnut brown foal, all arms and legs. He had an angular, oval face that tapered to a pointed chin. His dark eyes cast down on the floor, and he blushed red with the embarrassing question.

"Alcohol poisoning," said LeCroix. "He inflated his liver."

The young man didn't look up as he scribbled with his pencil in a notebook. Then he backed up, trying to get out of the way of the reporters and at the same time pressing himself against the wall.

"Now, if you'll excuse me." LeCroix walked through the scrum and across the lobby. He glanced back at the young man, while another reporter hit the embarrassed young man on the shoulder and said something to him.

Then someone bumped into him.

"Sorry!" said a boy, then kept running into the lobby and out the door. Two other people were running down the hall. LeCroix threw himself against the wall, out of their way. One man had stopped at the top of the hallway, leaning on his knees, gasping for breath.

"What's going on?" LeCroix demanded of someone, anyone.

The man looked up, then down, shaking his head. "Kid ... stole wallet."

LeCroix frowned and walked up the hall.

2

LeCroix walked out of the room of the man laying prone in bed. LeCroix had done the normal bleeding practice, but still the man's face was swollen. He had also taken out three offending teeth, all to no avail.

The man's wife sat downstairs in the kitchen, already wearing black. Three small children were in the kitchen, one washing dishes, the other two too young to do any chores yet.

"I've bled him. We'll see how long it goes on. I can come back tomorrow."

The wife shook her head. "We can't afford it." She got up. She looked exhausted, and LeCroix felt pity. But he had a job to do, and he had to get paid, or he didn't live. He wasn't like Dr. Kuchner, who lived in one of the mansions up north and charged his patients more than they could afford. A doctor was expensive under the best of circumstances.

The wife took down a small porcelain sugar holder from the top shelf of her cabinet. "How much?"

"Ten cents." He pulled out his small purse from his doctor's bag and she dropped the two nickels into the purse. "Please let me know how he is tomorrow. If he's worse, I have an elixir that may put him back on his feet."

She said nothing, escorting him to the door. He carried his black leather bag and stuffed it into the saddlebags of the horse he had tied up out front. He opened his notebook and wrote down in it under today's date:

Tomas Perreault. Visit tooth. Swollen face. Bleeding. .10 cash.

He next had to see Mr. And Mrs. Voisin, to make sure they had a baby that was healthy and Mrs. Voisin was out of childbed. Not that he didn't trust the midwife, Pelagie, but this was a courtesy call predicated by Mrs. Voisin's mother-in-law's belief that Pelagie was a witch and put some spell on the new child so that it wouldn't thrive.

3

LeCroix clicked the horse out of the yard and pointed its head toward the southeast. As the horse walked, LeCroix wondered whether he should have healed the man. It was obvious to him that he was the only one running the farm — the wife probably couldn't read. He had healed other farmers before, but it took a lot out of him, and he had become to be known as a miracle worker. But he didn't know what was causing the man's swollen face, other than possibly the bad teeth. If he knew what caused the issue, he could heal it.

His doctoring was different than modern day work. While other physicians believed in the disequilibrium of the body, he carried beliefs from the Middle Ages, when he was first trained as a physician. Most physicians these days did only the bleeding. He had elixirs to promote or demote the different Humours. He suspected an infection, which meant the Yellow Bile was too high, and this meant he needed to sweat the man out.

As he thought about what the next treatment should be, he saw a pack of Union soldiers coming his way. The Battle of New Orleans had happened only a couple of weeks ago, and the Union conquered the city without razing it to the ground. LeCroix worked as a surgeon for the Confederates, and he was lucky that the Union soldiers let him still stay in business. He had worked in New Jersey, when it was first settled, under the name of David Cross, before the Union had dispensed with slavery and became the progressive abolitionists they were now.

LeCroix tipped his hat as he approached the men. "Gentlemen," he said.

One man held his hand up and they all stopped in the middle of the road. "Where are your papers?"

LeCroix stifled a sigh and tucked a hand in his vest pocket. He pulled out a folded piece of paper that proved his name and his profession. "Where are you headed?"

"The Voisins. Checking on their new baby."

"You're the surgeon." The soldier folded the paper and handed it back to him.

He said it like it was a curse. "I'm a physician." He tucked the paper back into his pocket.

"Same thing," said the soldier. "Where did you come from?"

"The Pereaults. Tom's sick."

The Union soldiers looked at each other. A few grinned. "We'll have to pay a visit," said the man, and led the men forward.

LeCroix watched them go, and debated whether he should have said anything. He knew that by himself he couldn't do anything to stop the Union soldiers, but maybe someone else could. He turned down the nearest lane and stopped at the house at the end. He tied the horse to the pole for that purpose and walked up the veranda steps. He was familiar with who lived in this house, and knew he had three sons.

A slave woman answered the door.

"Where is the man of the house?"

The slave stepped aside and let him in. She went upstairs, and a broad man came down.

"Dr. LeCroix. What brings you here?"

LeCroix stood with his hat in his hand. "Sorry to disturb you, Mr. Lavolier, but I just came from the Pereaults. Tom's sick, and some Union soldiers are heading there."

The man frowned, which made him look angry. "Albeit for ulterior motives, no doubt. Hannah, fetch my gun and tell Morris to get John and Joseph and three horses ready for travel."

Lavolier walked out to the porch. "We can take care of this," he said.

"I don't want to have to come back to take a bullet out of you, Mr. Lavolier."

He laughed. "The gun is for show."

LeCroix got on his horse, feeling confident that they would watch out for Mrs. Pereault, and went to the Voisins.

4

When LeCroix got home, his slave Theodolus stood outside the door with a lantern. LeCroix dismounted in front of the door.

"Anyone call while I was gone?"

"Elizabeth has the names, Master David."

LeCroix nodded and went in by the front door while Theodolus took the horse to the stable in the back. He walked inside, smelling something cooking from the kitchen. He smiled and sat down to take off his boots. Elizabeth, a large, well-fed slave, came down the small hallway from the kitchen, wiping her hands on her apron.

"Master David, have you had dinner?"

"No," he said. "I'm going to wash up first. Tell me who stopped by."

Elizabeth took out a piece of paper from the folds of her skirt. "Mrs. Ortega says her son has a rash that she doesn't know where it came from. Mrs. Dessaline for her husband's grandmother who has taken a turn. Mrs. Augustine for women troubles. Sergeant Tillinghast for bullet wounds. Mrs. —"

"Wait, a sergeant for bullet wounds?"

"Yes, Master."

He looked at the clock. "I'll see him first thing tomorrow."

He walked past Elizabeth to a pitcher and basin. He poured some of the rosewater into the basin and washed his face and hands. He toweled off and heard a knock on the door.

Elizabeth opened it. "Is Dr. LeCroix in?" a man asked.

"Yes," LeCroix called. "Who's there?"

The man came in. "Sergeant Tillinghast."

"You came earlier. What's wrong?" LeCroix walked over to the foyer.

The sergeant leaned heavily against the door frame. "I need a doctor."

The man looked in his early twenties. He had dark hair and blue eyes, with a thin, lithe, almost feminine frame. LeCroix beckoned to Theodolus.

"Help him to the dining room. Elizabeth! I need some boiling water."

He retrieved his doctor's bag from near the kitchen door where Theodolus had placed it after getting it from the horse. He brought his instruments into the dining area, while Elizabeth set out a pan of hot water. LeCroix dropped his instruments into the boiling water and used a wooden spoon to move them around. It was a trick he had learned in Venice to stop infection.

"Where's the injury?" LeCroix asked as he put the instruments in the water.

The man glanced at Theodolus. He turned around, and pointed to just below his buttocks. The fabric there had markings of dried blood.

LeCroix didn't want to know how he got shot there. "You'll have to drop the trousers, Sergeant," he said.

Elizabeth went into the other room. Theodolus stood by. Tillinghast stared at the slave.

"Does he have to be here?"

"I'll need him to aim a light at the area if I can't see it," said LeCroix.

The man sighed, and undid his trousers. He pushed them down with a grunt. LeCroix dropped to his knees to better examine the area.

LeCroix wore his physician's hat for the moment, trying to ignore the smooth, creamy thighs and instead look at the wound. It was deep, and would not be easy to get at, even with ether. There were different ways to go about getting the bullet out, which included digging at it with pliers and tweezers, making the wound larger, and trying to pull the ball out.

Or there was always his knack. He could use the blood to push the bullet out.

"Theodolus," said LeCroix, "get this man some of my good whiskey. He's going to need it."

Tillinghast's eyes widened. "What are you going to do?"

"Well, there are two options: I sew this up and you walk around with the bullet in you and in pain, or I dig it out causing excruciating pain now but easing the pain later."

"I don't need the whiskey," he said, watching Theodolus go to the liquor cabinet.

"Now is not the time to be a teetotaler," said LeCroix.

"Sew it up."

"You may have hit the bone in your thigh, which is why you can't walk on that leg."

The man turned to face him. This time LeCroix studied the man's body. He was smooth, down to his member, uncut and of a good length, even while flaccid. His testicles hung lower, covered with fine hair, colored darker than the hair on his head. His thighs were thin, not overly muscular.

He snapped his eyes up to Tillinghast's face. Tillinghast was looking down at him. LeCroix looked down to see that Tillinghast was beginning to swell.

He had his back to Theodolus, and LeCroix was still on his knees. LeCroix said, "Theodolus, go to the kitchen and wait there until I need you."

"Yes, Master," said the black man, going into the kitchen. LeCroix heard the door close. He risked a glance at Tillinghast's member. It had, indeed, grown larger in just the few moments he was there on his knees. LeCroix reached out with his hand and hefted the growing cock.

Tillinghast exhaled sharply. He didn't pull away. LeCroix moved his head forward, and licked around the foreskin covering the head of his member. Tillinghast moaned, as his hand dropped to LeCroix's head. LeCroix used his tongue to push the foreskin away, and began lapping at the head.

"Oh, God," Tillinghast whispered, slowly rocking his hips, feeding him a little more each time. LeCroix felt the man's hand on the back of his head start to push him forward, and he opened his mouth a little wider. Tillinghast slipped into LeCroix's mouth, pulled back slightly, and then thrust again forward. LeCroix dropped his hand down to his own crotch, squeezing his hardening member through his pants. He moaned, even while Tillinghast started to thrust a deeper.

Tillinghast kept LeCroix's head still as he thrust, while LeCroix tightened his lips around the throbbing member. LeCroix finally unbuttoned his trousers and pulled himself out, again moaning around Tillinghast's cock. Tillinghast cast his head back at the feeling that moan put through him.

"Oh, God, yes, God ..."

LeCroix stroked himself, as Tillinghast thrust forward with a grunt and exploded in his mouth, filling it with white cream. LeCroix swallowed as fast as he could, feeling the pulsing of the man's cock in his mouth as it spasmed. LeCroix stroked himself relentlessly, pounding his own cock in his hand. When Tillinghast pulled back, he was still stroking himself, gazing at the cock he had brought to fruition, a cock that was even still hard, even while the man panted and slowly released LeCroix's head.

LeCroix lay his cheek against the hot, wet member, and licked its shaft. Then he gave a short "Oh!" cry, and shot along the hard woods of his floor. He mouthed Tillinghast's member as he spasmed in his hand.

Tillinghast looked down at LeCroix and smiled. "That was unexpected."

LeCroix panted and lay his head against the man's thigh. He waited for the lights behind his eyes to go out before saying, "You'll pay less, now."

Tillinghast chuckled. "I guess you'd better sew me up."

"There's another option. It will hurt, but not as much."

"All right," said Tillinghast.

"Bend over the chair."

Tillinghast did, exposing his buttocks. *Another time, perhaps*, LeCroix thought, again putting on his physician's hat. After stuffing himself back into his pants, he examined the wound, and put his hands on either side of it. He could visualize the *minie* ball, pressing against the thigh bone. Blood gathered around it. Muscles loosened and relaxed as he pulled blood from them.

It took some time for the blood to fill the area and begin to push the ball out. When it did, it slipped out of the wound and fell to the floor. Tillinghast began to bleed copiously all over his leg and the floor.

LeCroix grabbed the nearest placemat and put it against the wound, all the while willing that the blood stop flowing. When that placemat was saturated, he grabbed the edge of the tablecloth and used that.

"I feel dizzy," said Tillinghast.

"A moment, I'll have you sewn up and then you will stay for dinner."

"I have to get back before curfew," he said.

"Did you ride or walk?"

"Walked."

LeCroix looked at the clock. It was approaching curfew. He hated to send the man on his way with this much of a loss of blood. "You'll be walking like a drunken man."

"I'll be fine," he said. "Is it done?"

"Let me get you sewn up." He took out his needle and suture, and started to sew the wound closed. He put a bandage on it, brushing the man's testicles as he reached between his legs to wrap it around his leg.

Tillinghast turned around quickly, grabbing a hold of the edge of the table as he did. He wavered slightly. "I should sit down."

He dropped into the chair as LeCroix yelled, "Elizabeth! Get me bread and jam."

Tillinghast looked pale. Elizabeth came into the room carrying a tray, hesitating for a moment at the mess. LeCroix took the tray from her hands, placing it on the table. He spread some jam from the crock onto the roll and handed it to Tillinghast, who took it and ate it slowly. "That should help."

The sergeant nodded. LeCroix stood over the sergeant, watching, concerned. Tillinghast finished the bread while Elizabeth gathered the blood-stained placemat and cloth from the table.

"Are you sure you can make it back?" asked LeCroix.

"It's only the city hall," he said. "It's not far from here."

Less than half a mile, LeCroix thought. Tillinghast rose, putting on his pants, careful to ease it over the bandage. "I appreciate this."

"My bill," said LeCroix, looking for a pen and paper.

Tillinghast said, "I'll collect it tomorrow."

"This same time tomorrow."

Tillinghast nodded. He put on his Union cap, and limped to the door. Theodolus let him out into the night.

LeCroix sat down as Elizabeth put a new table cloth on the table. "I don't know if I'll be able to get the blood out."

LeCroix waved a hand. "We have linens. I'll take my dinner now."

He glanced at the door. He hoped the sergeant would come back.

5

The next morning, as he was getting ready for his rounds, he saw some Union soldiers walking with a Negro down the middle of the French Quarter. LeCroix didn't know the colored man, but Mrs. Ortega did.

"He raped a white woman," she said when she let LeCroix into her house.

"Who did?"

"That Negro."

"They'll hang him and be done with it." LeCroix shrugged. "What's this about your son?"

After seeing to her son's rash with a poultice, he went to the other people on his list in his notebook. He made a circular route, starting from the French Quarter where he lived, out toward the rural areas in the outskirts of the city, places where the other rich doctor wouldn't go. While that rich doctor was paid with money, LeCroix was paid with food and labor. He found that to be more rewarding.

As he left the French Quarter, heading north, he saw the Negro man hanging by his neck from a tree, a black bird pecking out his eyes. Even though the Union and their progressive ideas had come to Louisiana in May, they still at least understood southern justice.

LeCroix ended up back at the Perreaults, but no one answered the door. Curious, he went to their nearest neighbor, the Cormiers. There were a few horses outside, more than usual, and a carriage. He went to the door, and a young lady answered it.

LeCroix smiled. "Miss Cormier."

She curtsied. "Dr. LeCroix."

"What's going on?"

"Mrs. Perreault is here. She was attacked."

"Attacked? When?"

"Yesterday."

Miss Cormier was a pale girl, not like the tomboy she had been a couple of years before. She wouldn't have been caught dead in a dress, but now, with the prospects of her having to get married, she had to constantly present herself as a young lady in case of handsome callers. And LeCroix happened to be one of them, as he well knew. She stepped aside and let him into the house.

"Is she hurt?"

Miss Cormier bit her lip. "She's being seen to."

A scream ripped through the house, one of pain, and then loud noises of vomiting. LeCroix looked upstairs, then back at the girl.

"Please find out if I should go see her."

The girl swished her dress and, lifting it, walked slowly up the stairs.

Another scream of pain.

A group of men came out of a side room. Cormier, Lavolier, and the senior Voisin were among the men there — the old men of the plantations outside of the city, the richer men.

And so was Dr. Kuchner. He was a small man, coming up to most of the other men's chins, dressed all in black like an undertaker. He carried his doctor's bag of the finest leather, small and compact as opposed to LeCroix's saddlebags that nearly bulged with all his instruments. He had curly black hair, a large, bulbous nose, and glittering black eyes that reminded LeCroix of the Orthodox men of Brooklyn, New York. Except he didn't wear a skullcap.

"*Doctor* LeCroix," sneered Kuchner, looking down his nose at him. "What a surprise."

"What's going on?" Miss Cormier came down the stairs as if the hounds of hell were after her.

"She's in good hands," said Kuchner. "Her husband was killed and she was, it seems, attacked."

"Killed? I saw him yesterday."

"Killed in his bed," said Lavolier. "By the time we got there, he was already dead. Shot." He placed his hands behind his back. "We found Mrs. Perreault in the barn. Assaulted."

Assaulted when applied to a woman usually meant anything from a slap in the face to rape. He assumed the latter.

"I've given her a purgative," said Kuchner. He glanced at the men. "I assume the husband's body will be disposed of?"

Cormier said, "I'll send some women to prepare the body."

"It will be a sensitive scene," said LeCroix. "Especially if he was shot in bed."

"I deal with the living, not the dead," said Kuchner, pointedly looking at LeCroix. "If you gentlemen will excuse me?"

Another scream echoed, not as loud or as powerful as the first two. Cormier turned to the girl who was standing there, shaking.

"What do you want, Emily?"

"Mama wants Dr. LeCroix."

"I am not paying for two physicians," said Cormier.

"She may be screaming all night," said LeCroix. "If I know Dr. Kuchner."

Cormier sniffed. The screaming would get to him, LeCroix knew.

"Don't stay long. We need you to attend to Mr. Perreault."

He followed the girl upstairs, who looked even more pale. "She's bleeding. Everywhere."

LeCroix put a hand on the girl's arm. "I'll take care of it."

She led him to an open door. Women were gathered all around. Mrs. Perreault, sweating, in a thick, heavy black dress including corset, was lying on the bed. Vomit overflowed from a pan at the foot of the bed.

Mrs. Cormier was wringing her hands.

"Oh, Dr. LeCroix," she said. She was delicate like her daughter, her corset tightly tied so that she looked like a muffin with an overflowing top. "Can you stop her from screaming?"

Mrs. Perreault made a gurgling sound, and a matron lifted her up, aiming her toward the chamberpot at the foot of the bed. She made a loud roaring sound, but nothing came out.

"How was she assaulted?" asked LeCroix, immediately going to her. "Get her out of this dress and this corset. She can't breathe."

"But a man is here," said the matron. Her voice was thickly southern.

"Mama, this man is a doctor."

"A lady should always be presentable to a man."

"A lady should be healthy before that," LeCroix stated coldly. "Now get her out of this dress or I will do it myself."

The matron glared at LeCroix, a stare of death. LeCroix had seen that — and worse. He had faced a goddess of death, and this was nothing compared to Her.

"Turn your back," she ordered LeCroix, and he did that, looking out into the hallway. He heard moaning behind him, the rustle of fabric, and then nothing but breathing. He turned around to see them put the finishing touches on the duvet, pulling it up to her neck.

LeCroix said, "Please leave."

The matron gave him a shocked look, then stormed out of the room. Mrs. and Miss Cormier left the room, closing the door.

LeCroix shook his head. The chamberpot was on the floor where it belonged. Mrs. Perreault was still pale and shaking. "How are you feeling?"

"They killed Thomas."

"I know." He felt her head. No fever. "Who did?"

"Union soldiers," she said. "They ... they dragged me and Lilly out into the barn."

LeCroix hooked a chair from a vanity and sat down next to her. "What did they do?"

"They — they beat me, and then …" She turned her head. "They took their turn on Lilly. And …" Her voice was barely above a whisper. "Me."

LeCroix clenched his hands into fists. Those men, if he ever saw them again, would wish they were dead by the time he got through with them.

"I'm so very sorry."

"I don't want to have their baby, if they caught me. Lilly's too young."

"Do you want me to get Pelagie? She is well-versed in such women's problems."

"I won't have anything to do with that witch," she said angrily. "Dr. Kuchner gave me a purgative."

"Yes, but even Dr. Kuchner should know that the womb is not connected to the stomach."

At least, he thought he would know. LeCroix didn't have anything at hand that could purge the womb, but he supposed he could make something with the native plants of the area. He knew of something using French herbs — he would have to look it up to be sure — but those were plants native to France. He didn't know if the apothecary in this area would have access to the items he needed. He didn't have much time to do it in, though.

"But if you are pregnant, there is nothing that can be done but to carry the child."

"I will kill it after it is born. I don't want a Yankee brat."

"You can give the child up. I'm sure there are many childless —"

She turned away. LeCroix knew he had lost her.

"Maybe we can find the father."

She stiffened suddenly, and raised herself up from the bed, making sounds of vomiting, but nothing came up. She lay back down, panting.

LeCroix left the room. The women waited outside.

"Is she?" asked Mrs. Cormier.

LeCroix knew what she meant. "We will have to see after her moon," said LeCroix. "I can do nothing here."

"If she didn't have her own children, she would kill herself."

LeCroix said nothing, going down the stairs. The men had gathered outside on the porch, away from the screaming woman and her vomiting.

"She'll be fine," said LeCroix to their inquisitive looks.

"You will see to the body, LeCroix?" asked Voisin.

Kuchner could have, but the rich doctor wouldn't go near dead bodies. LeCroix was usually called in to do things like that.

"Tell Remy and have him meet me at the house." Remy was the carpenter who made coffins.

LeCroix rode to the Perreault's. When he entered the house, there were already black flies buzzing around the bottom floor. He climbed the stairs. Mice had gotten to the body and eaten out its eyes. LeCroix swallowed bile and set to work, examining the body for other wounds. Two shots to the head caused blood to pool under the body and sink into the mattress.

He cleaned the body as best as he could, when he heard, "Heyo!"

"Up here, Remy," called LeCroix.

Remy came upstairs, a handkerchief over his nose. "Ugh, what a stench!"

A large, broad shouldered man who had to step in sideways stepped into the room. He was just a little taller than LeCroix, with shoulder-length raven-black hair and a chiseled, square face. He was built all in his chest and shoulders, with a trim waist and short legs like most of his Cajun brethren.

"He's been here for a day or so," said LeCroix, covering the body with a clean sheet he found in the nearest wardrobe. He would dress the body in the man's finest suit before they would bring it downstairs.

Remy came up behind LeCroix. He pressed his body against him, and LeCroix felt the man's hardening member against the crack of his buttocks. LeCroix wasn't sure if seeing dead bodies did this to him, or if seeing LeCroix dd it, but this wasn't the first time this kind of thing happened.

LeCroix sunk backward against Remy, who nuzzled his face into LeCroix's neck.

"You smell better."

He licked at LeCroix's neck, up to his earlobe.

LeCroix shivered, his nipples hardening under his shirt.

"Remy —"

Remy moved his hands around to LeCroix's torso, unbuttoning the shirt.

"You say this all the time, David. You say, 'Not in front of the body.' There's no one here."

Remy parted the shirt, exposing his chest to the air. LeCroix took a deep breath, thrusting his chest forward into Remy's hands. He also pushed backward, against the now-hard cock in Remy's pants.

"You want it as bad as I do," Remy said. "This is the only time you get it the way you want it."

It was true, but he also liked to give as well as take. Nobody in the French Quarter knew of his want of men, though he assumed it was suspected since he lived alone. The few possibilities in the Quarter were like skittish horses, and ran away before he could actually proposition. Remy didn't need a proposition. He took what he wanted.

He forced LeCroix to bend over, his hands on the edge of the bed. Remy unbuttoned LeCroix's trousers, and pushed them down. Remy then just unbuttoned his pants, pulling out his own member, large, thick, and pulsing.

"What is the magic that you do?" he asked.

LeCroix concentrated. Remy watched as he leaked copiously over his head. He moaned, as he started to stroke himself, adding to the liquid.

"Ah, yes. You pull it out from me."

"Do it," said LeCroix, in his compromising position, avoiding looking at the body.

Remy placed his hands on LeCroix's hips, his member against LeCroix's hole, and he yanked LeCroix onto him. LeCroix yelped, as he always did, the size surprising him.

Remy relentlessly pounded LeCroix, while holding onto LeCroix's hips and guiding him in and out. LeCroix knew he was hard, as he bounced against his abs, but he refused to do anything to relieve himself. Not here. Not with a dead body here.

"Mercy," Remy said, and LeCroix stiffened, knowing this was the final thrust. Remy shoved himself deep within and grunted, while LeCroix could feel the wetness fill him, go down his leg. LeCroix looked up at the shape of the body on the sheet, and he shivered, but he didn't dare let himself go.

Remy let himself soften inside of LeCroix, then pulled out the last bit.

"Always worth it to come to help you with a body."

LeCroix turned to him, his member hard, sticking straight out. Remy looked down at it for a moment, and chose to ignore it. LeCroix forced himself to think of something else, anything other than Remy tucking himself back into his own pants. He thought of Perrault lying there dead in his own blood. That helped bring him down enough to stuff himself back into his pants.

Remy, meanwhile, went around to the side of the bed away from LeCroix and pulled out the sheet.

"You take the legs?"

"Yes," LeCroix said.

He pulled out the bottom half of the sheet tucked into the mattress and wrapped it up so he didn't have to touch the cold, stiff body. He went downstairs first, backing onto the porch to the casket that was on the ground next to the horse-drawn wagon. The two horses turned their noses up at the smell. LeCroix didn't blame them.

Remy poured the body into the casket. The body was a little too broad, but he stuffed it in there, anyway.

"They gonna hold a wake?"

LeCroix looked at Perrault's head. There were two neat holes in the man's forehead, but the back of his head was blown off.

"I guess they might want to have last rites," LeCroix said. "We'll need to get the priest."

"Where's the wife? Don't she have kids?"

"Sick," said LeCroix. He had to see Pelagie about an abortion. "Kids are too young."

"They're gonna lose this farm," said Remy.

LeCroix looked up at the house. That was probably true. He had no idea who would buy it, haunted as it probably was now.

"I'll go get the priest," LeCroix said, walking over to the horse. "Help yourself to the food, I guess."

"Don't mind if I do," said Remy, going back into the house.

LeCroix would not be surprised if he found that small jar that Mrs. Perrault kept the money in and would steal every last cent.

6

Pelagie lived in a shack outside of New Orleans. LeCroix had seen the priest, who immediately got his implements and promised to see Mrs. Perreault right after seeing to Mr. Perreault. LeCroix ducked under a large branch as he walked his horse along the path. Signs and portents that he knew from the very old days were etched into the trees or hung from branches along the well-worn trail.

Many women walked to this woman's shack, and she walked to many a woman's home. When he came out of the trail into the small cleared area of her shack, he saw three scrawny chickens running underfoot and two goats that bleated at him. Pelagie stepped out of her shack and peered at him.

"Cross," she said, and put her arms across her chest.

"Oh, what did I do now?" he asked her, as he dismounted.

"What's this about the Voisins?"

"Don't blame me, blame Margarite."

Pelagie snorted. "Tea?"

"I'd love some."

Pelagie let him into her one-room house. There was a banked fire, which she set a kettle on, and took out two stone cups without handles, putting herbs into each from jars along the rafters.

"Where did you come from that you smell like blood?"

"The Perraults. They were attacked. Mrs. Perrault was raped."

Pelagie *tsked* as she sat down onto a creaking stool. LeCroix sat across from her.

"So you've come here to be rid of the child?"

"Yes."

Pelagie looked at him steadily. "Or do you come here for a love potion?"

"Love potion?" He laughed, though he felt his face get hot, thinking of Tillinghast's creamy white skin.

"One is not too much further than the other."

"I don't think I need a love potion."

"As you wish." She glanced at the kettle. "But if you need one, I have a few."

"The purgative only."

She got up and got the kettle. The water was hot, not boiling, and she poured it into the stone cups. She also retrieved some shortbread cookies from a tin can. LeCroix didn't realize he was famished until he saw the food and ate three before he realized what he was doing. He forced himself to slow down.

"I never thought Ginny would want a purgative."

Ginny, he thought. Virginia. Mrs. Perrault. "She said she doesn't want a Union brat."

"She's a Catholic. They don't like things like that."

LeCroix shrugged. He was a Catholic in name only. He knew who his Goddess was. So did Pelagie.

When they first met, as adversaries, Pelagie's mother told him that he was a priest of Lilith. Of course he denied the accusations. No one paid attention to the madwoman anyway. Two years ago, Pelagie suddenly worked with LeCroix. She took him aside one day and told him, "Your

Goddess told me to help you, that this is your last life on Earth."

He had lived a long time and, sometimes, he was tired of it. He had lived through the Gauls and sack of Rome, the dark ages of France, the rise of Venice, the exploration of the Portuguese, the colonization of the New World. Many days, even in the arms of men, he was lonely, and had not felt the pull of his soulmate.

Until Tillinghast. He hoped Tillinghast would come back to his place with the money tonight. Maybe he could get him to stay out past curfew.

LeCroix shook his head while Pelagrie smiled, sipping her tea. "Are you sure you don't need that love potion?"

"I'm sure," he said.

He sipped the tea. It had finally cooled enough to drink. He thought again about Tillinghast, the first time he'd had a chance to rest.

Pelagrie rose and started putting together the purgative.

7

When he rode back to Voisin's house to bring the purgative, he passed through New Orleans' French Quarter. Spared by the Union army during the short-lived battle, there were still Union soldiers patrolling along its streets.

LeCroix was thinking about going to his home to pick up something to eat when he heard someone call him. He turned to see Sergeant Tillinghast trot up to him. He sat easily on the horse, as if he hadn't been injured at all. Behind him rode four men that LeCroix assumed were part of his patrol.

"Hello, Sergeant," said LeCroix. He glanced at the man's thigh. "How are you feeling?"

"Good. Are you going to be home tonight?"

"I plan on being home in a few hours."

LeCroix drew his eyes up to look at Tillinghast's face. He had a touch of a grizzled shadow along his jaw, that he hadn't shaved in a couple of days. His round face betrayed a baby-like look to him. LeCroix assumed the man was younger than even he himself appeared to be. A black lock of hair, the style of the time, crossed Tillinghast's forehead enticingly.

"I, uh, need to deliver this medicine." LeCroix smiled. "Would you like to come to dinner?"

"I would enjoy that very much," said Tillinghast. His eyes glanced at LeCroix's pommel, behind which he knew what he would have liked to see.

"Will they let you go?" LeCroix inclined his head to the four men milling about just out of earshot.

"I'll be there. Sunset?"

"Yes."

Tillinghast nodded, spurred his horse and went back to the four men. LeCroix watched him go, not even realizing he was grinning ear-to-ear.

8

He stopped quickly at home to give orders to Elizabeth to find the best cut of roast she could and prepare it "the French way" for him and his guest. Then he went to Mrs. Perrault, who was sleeping, finally. He left off the purgative and headed home.

He got home before sunset and ordered up a bath. As he sunk into the hot water with a satisfied sigh, he wondered about Tillinghast again. He hoped he could bring Tillinghast to his bed. The thought of it caused him to swell in the water, and the comfort of the heat of the water made him even harder.

No, he thought to himself. He would save it until he saw him. And then, the two of them would lay together in his warm bed after a wonderful dinner.

He finished dressing when the doorbell rang. LeCroix passed his hands through his hair to comb it, and glanced at himself in the mirror. Yes, he needed a shave, but it was too late now for that. Smiling, he came down the stairs to see a boy in a Union uniform at the door.

His smile faded. "Can I help you?" he asked, trying to keep his voice flat.

The boy thrust out a piece of paper. It had been folded simply in half, so that the boy could have read it if he wanted to. LeCroix took the paper, nearly snatching it out of his hand. A dollar floated out from the folded piece of paper and onto the floor.

Theodolus bent and picked it up while LeCroix read, "Please accept my kindest regrets for this evening. This should be enough for last evening's work. Sincerely, Sgt. George Tillinghast, Massachusetts Militia."

He looked up to see the Union boy had disappeared.

"Dammit," LeCroix snapped, and slammed shut the door. He stomped into the dining area, throwing the letter down. Theodolus, carrying the dollar bill as if it was gold, lay it carefully on top of the letter. LeCroix dropped down into the chair and glowered at the letter.

He wasn't going to let Tillinghast go that easily.

9

The next morning, LeCroix went to the same area that he saw Tillinghast the day before. He ate breakfast at one of the cafe's there and stayed, even though he had rounds to make.

His patience was rewarded, when he saw Tillinghast, walking with about a dozen men, heading toward the city hall. LeCroix got up and followed them. A young man fell into step with him.

"Dr. LeCroix?"

"Yes?"

The young man smiled. "I'm Gerard Rabideau from *The Delta*."

"And you know me, how?"

"You knew Sebastian Audet. He's my first cousin."

LeCroix knew him more than just socially. However, it was a passing fling and both men knew it.

"I heard he died."

"Yes, sir, I'm afraid he did." Rabideau pointed to the Union soldiers walking into the city hall. "Are you going to see General Butler speak?"

"That wasn't my intent," said LeCroix.

"What was your intent?"

"I'm trying to get some money out of one of the men there for a surgery I performed."

Rabideau laughed. "Good luck with that. These Yankees don't pay their debts."

"They probably say the same thing about us."

"I'm going inside," said Rabideau, after they got to the bottom of the stairs. "I heard a rumor that the Yankees were going to pass a new ordinance."

"Probably some abolitionist nonsense," said LeCroix. He shrugged and went inside.

He noted Tillinghast inside the general assembly room, standing at attention while men surrounded the place. "The Beast" Butler, who lead the Department of the Gulf. He was a tall, slightly heavy man, stuffed into his blue Union uniform, his gold buttons shined to a bright sheen. He had long brown hair that disappeared from his forehead.

He stood at the podium, and issued his proclamation. It was a repeat of the proclamation he had already issued in the newspapers at the time, plastered all across the New Orleans Bee. LeCroix wasn't paying attention, instead looking at Tillinghast.

Look at me, he commanded silently in his mind. He wished sometimes that he had the ability of his Brothers of Air that could place a thought in a man's mind and force them to attend to it. Tillinghast stubbornly refused to look up in the gallery, his eyes straight forward and his body rigid.

Finally, after a half an hour, Butler finished. The Union soldiers disbanded in order, and LeCroix ran downstairs to try to catch Tillinghast again. LeCroix stood at the side of the building, along with another mob, that stood silently as the Union soldiers marched by. Tillinghast was with the group of marching men, and turned to face him. LeCroix watched him intently as the man nodded, then snapped his eyes front and marched out of the city hall.

LeCroix trudged back to his home.

10

"I'm surprised you work on the Sabbath," said Mrs. Blake as LeCroix sewed up her son's gaping wound from an axe.

"Only in emergencies, and I'm sure God would understand."

LeCroix tried not to look at the man's muscular body stuffed into the calico shirt, but the muscular calf before him was almost too much to bear. As long as he concentrated on the stitching, he would be fine.

"You need to keep this clean," said LeCroix, tying off the stitch. "Come back in a week. It should heal by then."

There was a knock on his door. Theodolus answered it. LeCroix didn't see who it was, as Mrs. Blake paid out his fee.

LeCroix cleaned up after the mother and son left, and looked up to see who Theodolus allowed into his house. His heart leapt.

"Sergeant," LeCroix said, keeping his voice level.

"Doctor LeCroix." The sergeant inclined his head. "I was wondering if you were busy."

He looked beyond Tillinghast to Theodolus. "Theo, you and Elizabeth can have the rest of the day off."

Theodolus grinned. "Thank you, Master," he said, and went into the kitchen to tell Elizabeth.

"Tea?" asked LeCroix, gathering up his instruments.

"Yes," said Tillinghast.

He sat down across from where LeCroix was stationed. LeCroix packed his bag and went into the kitchen.

Elizabeth left cold beef and potatoes on the stove. LeCroix heated up the kettle. He stood over the stove and heard the door to the kitchen open. Tillinghast stood in the doorway. He walked over to LeCroix and stood in front of him.

LeCroix leaned forward and kissed him. Tillinghast opened his mouth to receive him, and their kiss turned hungry and passionate. Lecroix reached down for Tillinghast's butt and grabbed him roughly, pulling his groin into his own, grinding against him. Tillinghast moaned. LeCroix could feel Tillinghast's member pressing against the uniform.

"I couldn't get away," Tillinghast said, spreading his hands across LeCroix's chest. He slowly began unbuttoning the man's shirt.

"You're here now," LeCroix said, thrusting his chest outward. Tillinghast parted the shirt, groping LeCroix's pectorals.

"To hell with the tea," LeCroix said, kissing Tillinghast again. "Come upstairs."

LeCroix moved the kettle from the stove, and rebuttoned his shirt awkwardly as they exited the kitchen. He climbed the stairs, checking back to make sure Tillinghast followed.

Tillinghast did follow, and the two men went to the bedroom. It was warm up here, cozy. LeCroix drew the curtains closed. Tillinghast stood in the center of the room, looking around the furnishings, the bookcases and the fireplace, not being used because of the warmth of spring. The bed was unmade, a tangle of sheets and blankets on a featherbed.

LeCroix returned to Tillinghast and started to slowly unbutton his military uniform. He kissed Tillinghast as he did so, pushing aside the uniform shirt, his hands pushing along his gray homespun cotton shirt to get the uniform off. It dropped with a thud to the hardwood floor.

Tillinghast took a deep breath, and LeCroix looked at the undershirt. "I should give you more shirts. How long have you had this shirt?"

He laughed. "Years."

LeCroix pulled the shirt up, out of the waistband. It barely held together as he tugged the shirt over Tillinghast's head. "I will give you another one."

Tillinghast smiled. He unbuttoned LeCroix's shirt and his hands fanned across LeCroix's chest. The two men groped each other's chest and embraced, their kiss rougher and more demanding. Tillinghast ground his hips against LeCroix's groin. Both men moaned.

LeCroix parted, chuckling. "Let me check your wound," he said. "Go lie down."

Tillinghast went to the comfortable featherbed and stretched out across it. LeCroix took a hold of the other man's belt and undid it. Then he slowly unbuttoned Tillinghast's pants, slipping them over his waist and butt while he groped at his ass, squeezing hard and lifting the man's hips up. As the pants slipped off, his erection popped up laying against his abdomen.

"Oh, yes," whispered LeCroix, and shoved the pants down. He took off the man's boots, glancing at the man's darned socks, and he smiled. He tugged off the socks, dropping them into the boots, while his cheek rubbed against Tillinghast's cock.

"Suck me again," said Tillinghast.

"Better," said LeCroix, and he unbuttoned his own pants, pushed them down. He climbed onto the bed, and lay with his head at Tillinghast's crotch, while his own cock, tip leaking, was at Tillinghast's mouth.

Tillinghast flicked his tongue up and licked at the pre-cum. LeCroix lowered himself down. Tillinghast opened his mouth and took in the head, licking and sucking at it. LeCroix also put his own head down onto Tillinghast's member, licking from base to tip.

LeCroix controlled how far down he went on Tillinghast, thrusting forward a little at a time, while he continued to lick and suck at Tillinghast's hard, throbbing cock. Tillinghast was not awkward, as LeCroix had expected; he used his fingers to tease at LeCroix's hole, even while he shoved LeCroix further into his mouth, hungrily taking him down. LeCroix surrendered himself up to the moment, letting Tillinghast guide him forcefully.

He felt his balls tighten, and he worked harder at Tillinghast's cock, bobbing his head up and down, moaning at each downstroke. He gripped the sheets and thrust his head forward, forcing him down further and further.

Then Tillinghast stiffened, his cock grew for a moment in his mouth. LeCroix lifted his head and let the man cum all over his face and sheets as he groaned, his mouth still on LeCroix's cock. He shoved LeCroix out of his mouth and LeCroix felt the chill of the air on his cock, but that didn't stop him from shooting on Tillinghast's face.

After a few moments, LeCroix went to his basin and took off the towel from there. He cleaned his face off, then handed it to Tillinghast.

Without any other words, LeCroix climbed into the bed and wrapped his arms around Tillinghast, slowly exploring the younger man's body with his hands for two hours. LeCroix fought off sleep, but Tillinghast dozed off.

An hour before dusk, he dressed the young man and escorted him downstairs. Theodolus and Elizabeth were nowhere to be found, which, LeCroix thought, was good.

"Next week?" asked LeCroix.

"Possibly," said Tillinghast.

Tillinghast led the way down from the study and paused in front of the mirror at the front door. LeCroix held Tillinghast's cap in his hand. He straightened his uniform and turned to LeCroix.

"Maybe next Sunday," he said. "Or earlier."

"Hopefully earlier," said LeCroix. He handed the cap to Tillinghast.

He placed the cap on his head. "Thank you."

LeCroix smiled. "Thank *you*."

Tillinghast returned the smile, opened the door and walked out. LeCroix sighed when the door closed after the young sergeant.

He retired to the kitchen and had the cold beef with some bread, then went to his study and read.

II

The next morning, he was awakened by pounding on the door. It was still dark. Theodolus answered the door while LeCroix got out of bed.

"Dr. LeCroix is still asleep—"

"Who is it, Theo?"

"Mr. Voisin's servant."

"Is it Mrs. Perreault?"

"Yes, sir," said a boy's voice. "She's bleeding."

LeCroix came down the stairs. "Saddle the horse. I'll be there shortly."

He washed his face and got himself dressed quickly in yesterday's clothes, then met Theodolus outside. Voisin's slave had run in the dark, not even using a horse. LeCroix hoped to overtake him and get to the house before he did.

He had learned the hard way not to gallop in the pre-dawn hours through the streets. Out in the fields, he had the light of the moon to guide him, so he let the horse run. He saw the house, all the lights burning in the windows, people running in and out from the front door.

LeCroix dismounted and grabbed his bag from the sweating horse. He got to the top of the steps, when a man stopped him from entering.

"I'm a doctor," he said to the man. The man was in shadow, so he couldn't see his face. He stood with his arms crossed, barring the doorway. "Let me pass."

The man said nothing. LeCroix stepped back a moment and studied him. He had a large, broad chest, wore a light shirt and dark pants, but LeCroix couldn't tell much else. But his body shape was familiar.

"Thomas?" LeCroix asked quietly.

There was a yell from upstairs, a woman's cry of anguish. The man turned his head to look behind and up, then stepped away from the door and deeper into shadow. LeCroix dashed into the foyer as a woman in a nightgown rushed down the stairs. LeCroix moved out of her way and started up the stairs. He smelled the fresh blood before he got to the door.

Men and women were gathered at the door. LeCroix saw their looks. He was too late.

"She bled to death," said Mr. Voisin.

"Did you give her my purgative?" In other words, was he to blame?

Voisin looked at the woman, who stood silently crying. She shook her head. LeCroix glared at the woman, then pushed his way into the room.

The stench of blood filled the air, and the bedding was soaked. She hemorrhaged from her vaginal area, a serious miscarriage. Kuchner's medicine worked.

"Lady," he whispered, and looked up at the ceiling, the sky beyond. He prayed in his old tongue, hoping The Lady would bear her soul away. Mrs. Perreault was no longer suffering, but her three children would be orphans now.

He approached the body. He closed her open, unseeing eyes, and placed two pennies on them to keep them closed. He went to the door and opened it. Everyone except the slaves were at the door.

"Please come downstairs, sir," said one of them.

LeCroix went downstairs to Voisin's study. He stood holding a snifter of brandy. He was still impeccably dressed, as if he had just woken up and dressed formally at two in the morning. LeCroix knew he looked like he had slept in his clothes.

"Brandy, doctor?"

"Yes," LeCroix said.

Voisin poured him two fingers and handed over the glass. LeCroix knocked back most of it, letting it burn the back of his throat and down into his stomach. He had been surrounded by too much death these past few days.

"Thank you."

"I sent the boy to Kuchner," said Voisin with a frown.

"Kuchner doesn't work after hours," said LeCroix. "I always end up with his patients after dark."

Voisin pursed his lips. "I suppose I'll pay you," he said, and dipped a hand in the drawer of his desk. He pulled out two crisp dollar bills. "This should be enough."

"Who will take care of the children?"

Voisin shrugged. "I will pay a call to St. Mary's. They'll send them to the orphanage, I suppose."

"And the body?"

"Now that you have pronounced her dead, we'll clean the room and move her to a more suitable place."

Probably the barn, LeCroix thought. The brandy tasted like ash. He set down the half-empty tumbler.

"I had best be going." He turned from the man, and went to the door. "I suppose the Perreault's farm will be for sale." He turned back to Voisin.

"Are you thinking of moving to the country, doctor?" asked Voisin, almost sneering. The Perreaults were nearest to the Voisins, so it would be more than likely that Voisin would buy the land. LeCroix had done this kind of thing before, attempting to stop a greedy man from taking away someone's hard-earned land or building. It never turned out well for him.

"I'm not sure," said LeCroix. *Let him think I would, so he'll pay more than what it's worth.* "I just might."

He left the room, pocketing the dollar bills, and went back out to the foyer. The world was beginning to lighten up with the sunrise, but the candles in the windows were still lit. He stopped at the shadow of the foyer, where he thought he had seen Thomas Perreault in the doorway.

It wouldn't have surprised him if he saw him again.

12

The next evening, a sharp rap on the door woke LeCroix from a doze in the library. Theodolus answered the door. As LeCroix straightened up from his wing-backed chair in the study, he heard Theodolus yell up, "Sergeant Tillinghast, sir."

"Send him up," said LeCroix. The servants were not allowed upstairs. LeCroix, if he had trouble getting dressed, would descend downstairs to request help. LeCroix stood at the wing-backed chair as Tillinghast entered the room.

"Sergeant," said LeCroix.

"Doctor," said Tillinghast, as he entered, then shut the door.

LeCroix crossed the few steps to him, embraced him, then kissed him. Tillinghast opened his mouth as his tongue slid along LeCroix's, exploring each other.

Tillinghast started to undo LeCroix's shirt. "I don't have much time."

"Enough for what?" asked LeCroix, helping him. He shrugged out of the shirt while Tillinghast spread his hands across LeCroix's chest.

"To feel your skin against mine," said Tillinghast, undoing his military uniform clumsily. Underneath was another shirt, that LeCroix unbuttoned. "I want you."

LeCroix parted the shirt, and one hand went down to Tillinghast's groin.

"To do what?"

He squeezed the man's hard member through the rough cloth of the uniform.

Tillinghast moaned. "Inside me."

LeCroix raised an eyebrow. "You want me to do that to you?"

He nodded.

"Have you ever had that before?"

"Yes," he said, unbuttoning his pants. He pushed them down to his knees, while his member bounced up and stood straight out.

LeCroix wrapped a hand around it, his fingertips digging into the vein beneath. Tillinghast gasped. LeCroix kissed him lightly on the lips, and went to his desk. He had there a jar of thick cooking oil, for just this purpose. He retrieved his jar and a small towel.

LeCroix watched as Tillinghast assumed a position against the wing-backed chair, his hands on the armrests, his butt in the air, exposed. LeCroix stifled a moan as he walked around. Smearing his finger with the jelly, he teased at the man's hole before thrusting it in. Tillinghast pushed back against his hand, wanting more immediately.

"You have done this before," said LeCroix, and inserted a second finger.

"At West Point," he said. "One of the upperclassmen."

"You enjoyed it." A third finger, and Tillinghast spread his legs, moaning.

"Give it to me. I've been wanting it since Sunday. I wanted you to do it then … please."

LeCroix positioned himself behind Tillinghast, rubbing with his free hand the baby smooth, pearly white skin of the man's ass. He pulled out his fingers and placed the head of his cock against the stretched hole. With the lube and the preparation, he slipped easily inside.

"Ohhhhh," moaned Tillinghast, as he backed into LeCroix.

LeCroix took Tillinghast's waist and pulled him onto his member, slowly thrusting forward, but Tillinghast wanted him to go faster.

"More. All of you. All of it," he begged.

LeCroix obliged, thrusting forward and pulling out, then thrusting again. Soon, he was caught up in the rhythm. He watched as Tillinghast tucked a hand below him, and Tillinghast cried out as he touched his own member, stroking it just a short bit before shooting white ribbons onto the chair.

LeCroix felt the contractions on his cock, and then he, too, was shooting into the man's guts, hot and tight. LeCroix stood on shaking legs as Tillinghast pulled himself forward and off.

"I must ..."

"Must you?" asked LeCroix, as Tillinghast turned around to face him. LeCroix caressed the man's jaw.

"Sunday. I promise. Sunday. Again." He pulled up his pants and buttoned them.

LeCroix helped him get straightened out. The man took a deep, shuddering breath.

"Sunday, my love," said LeCroix.

Tillinghast jerked his head up. He burst into a smile. "Sunday."

13

Although it could be considered bad luck, LeCroix attended the funeral of Thomas and Virginia Perreault. The children were there with a nun who looked like she had eaten lemons for breakfast. Thomas had a brother who was in the war, so his sister-in-law and his other two sisters attended. Mrs. Perreault had no relatives in the area, so no one came to speak for her.

During the cotillion, LeCroix found himself seated next to Mrs. Lavolier and her daughter. She had loaded her plate with the finger sandwiches. Her daughter, thin as a rail — as opposed to Mrs. Lavolier who was as wide as the saddle chair — was picking some of the sandwiches off the plate and surreptitiously tucking them under the table. LeCroix looked down to see a mangy dog had found its way beneath the table and was the benefactor of the sandwiches.

He looked across the room to see Voisin Junior without his wife — that would have been bad luck if she had arrived with the new baby. Voisin Junior was talking with his father and the local attorney, Alexander Thibeault, the executor of the will, most likely. If Perreault had left a will.

"It's too bad that Mrs. Perreault died. Look at her beautiful children," Mrs. Lavolier was saying.

"You could always adopt them," said LeCroix.

Mrs. Lavolier gave LeCroix a stunned look. "Why, what would I do with them? It's up to his brother and sister to decide to adopt the children, not me."

"His sisters are spinsters, mama," said the daughter, who LeCroix knew was going to have her coming-out party soon. "Just look at them."

"It would be better for them to stay in the family."

As it was, the three children has been whisked away to a corner with the nun, who admonished them constantly. The boy had been crying and was now mewling in the corner, seated with his knees up to his chin, while his sisters sat prim and proper at the table. LeCroix knew they were in shock. It wouldn't hit them until they arrived at the orphanage, when they realized they would be separated from their brother, and possibly never see him again.

Part of him felt for them. He had seen many orphaned children in his lifetime. He had even adopted one or two as his apprentice. But the boy was too young and the two girls would not be taken seriously as doctors. No, he couldn't do anything to help them.

The daughter smiled at LeCroix while she took another sandwich. LeCroix smiled back, glanced at her hand as she tucked it under the table. Three sandwiches remained, and Mrs. Lavolier hooked an arm around her plate, protecting them.

LeCroix rose. "I have to go. There's someone I need to see."

"Of course, Doctor," said Mrs. Lavolier. "Oh, you will come to our ball this Friday evening, will you not?"

"Of course," he said, and bowed to the two women. "Excuse me."

He approached Thibeault, who was finally alone. "Alex."

Thibeault wiped his brow. "Hallo, David. Fine day."

He knew Thibeault well enough to cut right to the point. "About the estate."

"Not you, too."

"Voisin?"

"Of course." Thibeault nibbled on a sandwich. "They didn't leave a will, at least not one that we could find in the house. So it reverts to the Department of the Gulf. I'm sure they have other more important things to discuss than the disposition of someone's land."

"Should I retain you to put a brief in to request that they sell the land first to me?"

He chuckled. "They'll put it up for auction. But it could take months."

"Since you're one of the only lawyers left in town," said LeCroix, "I'm sure you'll hear of it."

"If you're interested, the Simons' land is going to be up for auction in a week. The last heir to it died in Gettysburg."

"How much land is there?"

"A full tobacco plantation. Slaves are still there, since they have no place to go."

"And the crop?"

"Fallow in the field right now."

"I don't have the time to oversee a tobacco plantation."

"So what makes you think you'll have time to oversee the Perreault farm?" Thibeault smirked at LeCroix.

"Their farm isn't integral to the city. They don't have to trade their wares. They're self-sufficient."

"Don't like depending on the Department of the Gulf to have the markets open?"

"You could say that."

Thibeault's smirk disappeared. "It won't be a few months."

"Just keep me in mind."

If he was going to live his last days on this Earth, he wanted to live them in comfort, and out on a farm in almost the middle of nowhere sounded like the perfect place to be.

14

LeCroix dismounted in the brightly lit courtyard between the barn and the mansion. Lavolier had spared no expense for his wife and daughter, it seemed, as the place was lit as if it was daytime. He passed his hat and coat to the checker and received a dance card.

He frowned. As if he was going to actually use it.

Women flirted from behind fans, as he walked by. He smiled at them all, knowing most of them from when they were mere babes. He was still considered an eligible bachelor in the city; a rich, eligible bachelor.

He ended up gathering with the other eligible bachelors, but staying in the dark corner where he could watch them. There weren't too many of them left in town. Most of them had gone to fight in the Confederacy. There were, of course, no Union men in the room.

Miss Lavolier did happen to spot him and sent her second to come to ask him for a dance. She was a young girl, probably about three or four years younger than Miss Lavolier, and not shy at all. He smiled at her, trying to place her.

"You're new here?" he asked her when she succeeded in getting him to fill out the dance card.

"I'm Tamra's cousin from Kentucky," she said.

"You don't look like you're from Kentucky."

She giggled, her brown curls bouncing. "Not all of us are inbred, sir." She smiled and left him chuckling.

As she negotiated her way back to Tamra Lavolier, his eye was caught by a commotion at the front of the ballroom. Coming into view was a group of men in blue, guns drawn as they stepped into the main ballroom. The musicians slowed down and stopped playing.

LeCroix studied the man leading the group, and realized he knew where he had seen the man before. It was the same man who had stopped him on the road to the Voisin's, on the day Thomas Perreault was killed.

LeCroix had no weapons, and he knew that the few men he was with had no weapons as well.

The man waved a hand forward and three Union soldiers came toward the gathered men.

"C'mon," one of them said in his Yankee accent. "Outside."

The group of just over half a dozen men were herded outside into the bright light of the lanterns. Slaves held the lanterns up in a semi-circle as one soldier stood on the porch, aiming a gun down at the men gathered at the foot of the stairs.

"This is intolerable," snapped Voisin, as he was also herded out to stand among the men. "Your commanding officer will hear about this!"

"Talk to him," said one of the Union soldiers. "You know you're all past curfew."

LeCroix jerked his head up when he heard the crash of glass. The soldier with the gun didn't turn around, but the one who spoke did. A woman screamed. One of the bachelors that LeCroix knew named Martin Petipas, put a foot on the step and the soldier with the gun aimed it right at him.

More crashes of glass. Another shout. Then two shots in succession. Petipas rushed the stairs, and the soldier with the gun stabbed him in the side with his bayonet.

Everyone backed off then, while LeCroix rushed to Petipas's aid as he fell backward from the stairs. He parted the man's jacket and shirt to try and see the wound through the gush of blood. He had to force Petipas to take his hand away from his side to see the nasty gash. Luckily, it hadn't penetrated his stomach, but it probably lacerated his liver or his kidney.

LeCroix hadn't brought any of his instruments, not thinking he'd need them. He looked up at the solider who looked with eyes of steel down at them.

"I need to get some suturing instruments or this man will die," LeCroix said.

The soldier shrugged. "He dies, he dies. He shouldn't 've come up here."

"What!" cried Voisin, struggling to get to the bottom of the stairs, but two men held him back.

One of the other Union soldiers came out. "Lots of pretty women in there," he said. "What're you gonna do about it?" He pointed his rifle at Voisin.

"Wait," said LeCroix, as Petipas was taking gasping breaths. "What do you want?"

The soldier shrugged.

"Let me talk to your sergeant."

"He's … indisposed." The soldier laughed.

LeCroix raised his hands. "Please, leave the women alone."

"We'll see." He nodded to the ballroom. "Get in there, get what you want, Roy."

The young soldier went inside, while the other soldier stood aiming their gun at them. LeCroix looked at Petipas who only stared at LeCroix with wide eyes.

"Am I going to die?"

"No," said LeCroix. "Please," he said to the soldier, "let me at least get some sewing needles."

"The women are busy, too." Again, the soldier laughed.

"This isn't funny!"

"What's going on out here," said the leader, coming out from the home with two men behind him. He was still buttoning his pants. "We're finished here. You're all under arrest."

"We have a wounded man here," said LeCroix.

"So what. Get these men tied up and we'll march them to the jail."

"March?" said Voisin.

"You should have known better than to stay out past curfew." The leader walked past the men. LeCroix could have reached out and tripped him, but he didn't. The leader turned and whistled.

"You," he ordered one of the slaves, "Go in the barn and get a rope big enough to tie all these men up in a chain."

The black man nodded and ran into the barn nearby. Petipas was helped up by the other men, while LeCroix wiped the blood from his hands on the grass. A slave came back with two lengths of rope, which the men were tied up by their wrists, with one end tied to a horse. LeCroix was too far away from Petipas, who looked pale in the light. Petipas was between two of the older men of the town, with Voisin and the Lavoliers taking up the rear.

Voisin said, "This is intolerable. Your superior will hear about this!"

"Someone shut that old man up."

One of the soldiers gagged him with a piece of rope.

The horses began walking away, while the women gathered at the windows of the ballroom. Some looked the worse for wear, and were holding onto each other as the men were led away.

15

The men were separated. LeCroix demanded to be with Petipas. However, LeCroix was put alone in a cell at the far end of a row of cells. He had a pallet and an already full chamber pot in the six-by-eight-foot cell.

LeCroix watched the sun travel across the ceiling from the cut-out bars high up in the wall. He could hear the men in the jail yelling for a while, and then, nothing.

LeCroix went to the bars of his cell and looked out. No one was directly across from him, but he tried to call to whoever was next to him. No one answered.

The sunlight passed over the ceiling. He had no food, no water. He had been in a situation like this before, a long time ago, when the Spanish had thrown him in prison thinking he was a Moorish spy. The Spanish prisons were harsh, much worse than this modern-age prison. In the Spanish prison, he got his water from the sweat off the stones, and was fed green, moldy bread — whenever they felt like feeding him.

His head knew he wouldn't be left alone, but he almost panicked as the sunlight started to fade. Once the sunlight ended, the rats would come out.

The door at the far end of the jail opened. Men yelled again for attention, but LeCroix could hear them walking the sound of their boots on the stones getting closer and closer to him. The man who had captured him last night, the one who was called Captain Mills, stood outside of the door.

"I'll take care of this one," he said. "Unlock the door."

The jail guard unlocked the door. Three men stepped inside. LeCroix was in no condition to take down all of them at once. He rose from his pallet.

"So," said Mills, undoing his pants. "I heard that you enjoy boys."

"I don't know where you heard that from."

"Word gets around in this city." The two men leered at LeCroix as Mills unbuttoned his fly. "You don't exactly hide it very well."

LeCroix kept his eyes up, looking at Mills' face. He wouldn't look down.

"How would it feel to be fucked by a man?"

LeCroix snorted. "You mean you?"

One of the men punched LeCroix in the head so hard he thought he saw stars. The man then got behind him and kicked him in the back of one leg. He fell to the hard floor with a grunt. He watched as Mills unbuttoned his fly, and then he jerked his eyes upward, watching Mills' face.

"Want some food and water? You'll have to have to satisfy me, first."

LeCroix looked at Mills' flaccid cock and then back up at Mills. "I'd rather starve," he said, jerking his head and body back from the stench that rose from Mills.

"Tell me this isn't what you want," Millis said, thrusting his hips forward. Again, LeCroix backed away.

Millis looked down at LeCroix and said, "Then starve, you will."

He rebuttoned his fly, and nodded to the two men. One of them hit him again before they all walked out of the cage, locking him again in the cell alone.

LeCroix did everything he could to stop himself from throwing up.

16

"I do apologize, Doctor," said Sergeant Tillinghast as he unlocked the jail door.

LeCroix looked up at his savior. He had been in the jail a full day, with no food or water, while the other men were retrieved by their wives or daughters. Petipas had died before his wife came to get him.

LeCroix wasn't sure whether he should be angry at the uniform, or happy that it was Tillinghast. LeCroix got shakily to his feet. Tillinghast helped him stand. "Are you going to make it?"

"No," said LeCroix. "I've had no food or water, and you expect me to just get on a horse and ride away?"

"Again, I apologize."

"I want to register a complaint."

Tillinghast said, "I will get you some water, first."

He guided LeCroix out to the barracks and sat him on a chair. He brought LeCroix some watered-down wine that went right to LeCroix's head, making him initially dizzy. He almost threw up the concoction, but surprisingly kept it down while Tillinghast listened to what had happened the night before. He left out what had happened immediately after getting to the jail, not knowing how Tillinghast would take it. "Who's Captain Mills's superior? I want to tell him."

"He's already been reprimanded," said a voice.

Tillinghast stood at attention. LeCroix saw that it was General Butler, the same general who had addressed the assembly with his proclamations. Up close, he was smaller than LeCroix, but with a barrel of a chest and long hair and beard. LeCroix stayed seated, more out of rebellion than illness.

LeCroix said, "He's also responsible for the murder of a man, and, by extension, the death of his wife."

Butler crossed his arms. "What's this?"

"He accosted me on the road. He headed to the house I had just left. The next day, I was told the man of the house was murdered and his wife and daughter raped."

Butler narrowed his pig eyes. "These charges are grounds for a court martial, if not hanging."

LeCroix raised his head. "Nevertheless, I make them."

"Is it only your word?"

"One of the men who was captured, Lavolier, went to the house with his sons to see. Maybe they saw your captain there."

Butler looked at Tillinghast. "Come with me, Sergeant," he said, walking to the door. Tillinghast gave LeCroix a helpless look before following the general.

LeCroix wasn't sure if he was to stay or go, so he stayed, taking another sip of the watered wine. He would have been happy with some hardtack and jerky to settle his growling stomach. But he didn't dare get up, because he wasn't sure if he was still needed.

A couple of Union men came into the room, staring at him warily. He was in no condition to put up a fight, and they could tell.

One of them asked him, "Who are you?"

"Dr. David LeCroix. Do you have any food?"

The two soldiers looked at each other and one of them went into his rations, pulling out a slice of hardtack. LeCroix gave thanks to the goddess and fell on it like a ravenous wolf, even though it was like eating wood.

When Tillinghast returned, he sported captain's bars and a broad smile. It was dark outside, past curfew, but Tillinghast said he would escort him back to his home.

"Do you feel fit to ride?" he asked, when they got outside. Tillinghast put his arm around LeCroix's shoulders and guided him to the stable.

"I'll feel fit to ride," LeCroix said, "if it means I go home."

"You will," said Tillinghast, and he ordered two horses to be saddled and made ready.

He had to be helped onto the beast and he tried to sit up straight, but he wanted so badly to lie down and sleep and eat at the same time.

They rode the short distance to the French Quarter. His home was dark, so he guided the horse through the small alley to the stable, where the slaves slept.

Tillinghast helped LeCroix dismount, and LeCroix rang a bell that hung near the stable door. He waited a few minutes, and Theodolus came out, wearing a long night gown. "Master David," he said, shocked.

Tillinghast stared at LeCroix for a moment. "You keep slaves?"

LeCroix only shrugged as Theodolus unlocked the back door, lighting candles within.

"I thought they were only your servants and assistants."

"I'm rich enough to have two slaves," said LeCroix. "I pay their upkeep."

Tillinghast frowned as LeCroix stood at the doorway.

He turned around to face Tillinghast. "Will I see you next week?"

"We shall see," said Tillinghast formally, as he mounted the horse. He took the reins of the other animal and led them out through the alley.

Elizabeth followed, dressed in a hastily thrown-on dress. "Master David," she said, "What happened to you?"

"I want food and a bath, in that order. Soup with hearty bones and beans."

As the slaves rushed to do his bidding, LeCroix wondered what the problem was with owning slaves.

17

It took two days, but he recovered, and was back on the road on Wednesday. Days, and then a week went by, and Tillinghast didn't return.

A proclamation came down from General Butler, stating that women who dared to protest the Union were considered to be "working women" and would be treated as such. Mrs. Ortega's daughter was one of the women arrested.

LeCroix was eating Sunday dinner alone when there was a knock on the door. He set down his utensils and answered it.

"Doctor?" said the young Union soldier.

"Yes."

"Dr. Harrison wants you."

"Who's Dr. Harrison?"

"You're a surgeon?"

"Yes."

"Please come with me."

"Who's this doctor?"

"Our militia's doctor, sir."

LeCroix pulled on a jacket, grabbed his bag, and followed the boy.

They walked to the barracks where the Department of the Gulf was billeted. Among the spacious homes, men were in tents on the lawns and in the back of the houses. LeCroix didn't come up this way very often, mostly because this was Kuchner's territory for the most part.

He went into one of the homes that was guarded by a soldier. No one was in the foyer — no slaves, no greeters — but he was guided to a large ballroom that had been converted into a hospital. Three rows of men in various conditions lay on beds; some moaning in pain, some staring up at the ceiling in shock, some sitting up with their legs or arms amputated. The smell was almost overpowering, of men who hadn't been washed for weeks, decaying meat, urine and feces. LeCroix took out a handkerchief and put it over his nose as the boy walked him through the room.

At the rear of the hospital was a sheet, and the boy parted it, peeked inside. "I've brought him, sir."

"Very good," said the man in a light English accent. "Bring him in."

The boy held the sheet open for LeCroix, who was slightly afraid of what he would find beyond. He saw a man in shirtsleeves with blue pants and leather boots, seated at a desk. A large wooden table was in front of him, some parts of the wood stained black with blood. LeCroix barely held down his lunch.

The man rose, holding out his hand. "I'm Dr. Harrison."

"Dr. LeCroix. What is going on here?"

"I've stated to General Butler that I'm in need of assistance. Your name was suggested."

"Assistance?" asked LeCroix, motioning with his head to the men. "You need more than that."

Harrison bristled. "Doctor, there is only so much I can do in the field."

"You're not in the field. You should have access to everything you need. Water and soap might be a good start." He still had the handkerchief over his nose as he spoke. "Besides, what about Kuchner? He lives just a short distance away."

"You will be staying here, of course," said Harrison.

"And who will take care of my house? My servants?"

"You will have to set them free."

"What!" LeCroix's anger overrode the smell of the place. "I've trained them and had them since they were young. You expect me to just get rid of them? Where will they go?"

"General Butler is going to make a proclamation within the next month that all slaves are to be free."

"Impossible."

LeCroix meant to turn from Harrison, but Harrison said, "The men out there will die."

"What makes you think I care about your soldiers?"

Harrison sighed. "I had hoped not to do this, but it seems I will have to force you into service. If you do not assist, then you will be arrested and put in jail, where I'm sure General Butler will allow you to rot for the rest of your days." He stepped forward, close to LeCroix. "And no captain will come to save you."

LeCroix's body did not stiffen. He refused to give away the fact that Tillinghast had anything to do with getting him out of prison before. He blinked slowly at Harrison, like a bull that had been hit between the eyes and didn't know whether to fall or rush. He took the first option.

"I will go home at night."

"I need you here."

"I *will* go home."

They glared at each other. "Be here at sunrise tomorrow."

"Agreed. Do you have a nurse or two?"

"No."

"Then get some. I can't work without assistance," LeCroix said. He threw the sheet open and strode out of the hospital, his eyes front, not looking at the suffering men he would have to deal with on the morrow.

18

"So you're the new doctor," said the Union soldier at the front of the hospital.

LeCroix had brought Theodolus with him. This wasn't the first time that Theodolus had played nurse to his ministrations, especially when it came to surgery and post-operative procedures. From what LeCroix remembered of that hospital, most of the men were amputees or something very like that.

"Get water and soap in a bucket," LeCroix told Theodolus. "We'll start at the far end."

"Yes, master," said Theodolus, walking up to the hospital. The Union soldier let him pass.

LeCroix had prepared himself with a makeshift mask to hide the smell; he tied a handkerchief soaked overnight in rosewater over his face and went into the room. He walked through the ballroom to the room in the back. Harrison wasn't there.

"Oh, hell," LeCroix spat. He smelled food, and realized that the patients were being served breakfast. He wondered who was doing the serving.

He stepped out of the back room and saw two young women, not much older than Levolier's daughter, helping a man sit up in his bed. His sheet was stained with blood and urine. The women didn't seem to be distracted by the smell.

"Excuse me," said LeCroix, and he helped the women sit the young man up.

The young man had a hallowed-out look to him, like he had seen too much horror.

One of the women said, "You're the new Union doctor?"

"I'm not a Union doctor," said LeCroix. "I'm from the French Quarter."

The girl slipped into French. "I'm Annette, and this is Louisa. This is our mother's house."

"Our mother's taken to the upper floors when the Union took over," said the other girl.

"And all our slaves ran away."

"I'm sorry," said LeCroix.

He saw that they had large stockpot of soup and they spooned some into a small bowl, no bigger than a teacup. It was mostly broth, without any meat in it. But it was warm. Some of the men had broken out hardtack and gnawed on that.

"Where is Harrison?"

"The other doctor? He left."

LeCroix clenched his hands into fists. "He left?"

"Last night."

"Dammit!" LeCroix yelled, and punched his thigh. "Damn him!" And damn himself for being so stupid.

The two women flinched away from him, but LeCroix didn't notice. He fumed, looked up and down the hospital rows. Did Tillinghast have to mention his name?

"Damn, damn, damn it all." He stormed up to the front of the hospital to the Union soldier guarding there. "Who's above this doctor?"

He shrugged.

"Where's General Butler?"

The soldier raised an eyebrow. "I don't know."

"Find someone who does!"

The soldier also flinched. LeCroix turned to the other soldier at the front door. "Take me to him."

"Sir, I need to —"

"I don't care. You take me to General Butler immediately." LeCroix grabbed the man by the arm and marched him down the stairs. "Where is he billeted?"

As they walked among the Union tents, LeCroix could see the men in various degrees of undress, in and out of uniform. Normally he would watch the men, but he was so determined that he didn't even notice them. He stopped in front of a huge mansion, with Union tents on the grounds.

The soldier said, "I think he's in here."

"Doctor," called a familiar voice. Tillinghast came toward him from the side of one of the tents on the lawn. He was in only shirtsleeves, suspenders and his pants, and was barefoot. "What're you doing here?"

"Your doctor left me with all your wounded," said LeCroix.

Tillinghast raised his hands. "I had nothing to do with it."

LeCroix still simmered, even though now he knew Tillinghast wasn't to blame. But who was? "Where is General Butler?"

"I'll get dressed and bring you to him."

LeCroix stood outside of the tent while Tillinghast finished getting dressed. Now in his blues, Tillinghast walked over to LeCroix and beckoned him. They walked together to the mansion's doors. No guards were at the doors, so they continued inside.

LeCroix looked around the mansion, noting that nothing seemed to have been touched — statuary, tapestries, and artwork were still intact. Tillinghast stopped outside a door and knocked.

"Enter," called a voice, and Tillinghast stepped inside, saluting. "Colonel. I have Dr. LeCroix to see the General."

The colonel he addressed had his uniform unbuttoned. A fat man, sweating in the relative oppressive heat of this inner chamber, he wiped his brow and looked at LeCroix. "What is he to see him for?"

"I want to know where Dr. Harrison is."

"Yes, he's been discharged." The colonel looked with his piggy eyes at LeCroix. "You're a doctor."

"One of only two local doctors," said LeCroix. "There's another doctor here that is probably better suited for this sort of field surgery that you —"

"No, no, your name was mentioned that you did surgery in the field," said the colonel. "By the man down the road. Kitchener?"

"Kuchner," said LeCroix, fury tinging his voice.

"Yes, yes, that's the name. He said you were an excellent surgeon." The colonel wiped his brow again. "It's only until we get a new surgeon. Depending on the blockade, it could be only a few months."

"A few *months*? What about my patients?"

"I'm sure Kitchener can handle that. He said he could." The colonel looked at Tillinghast. "Please escort the good doctor back to the infirmary."

"Yes, sir," said Tillinghast, saluting. He gently took LeCroix's upper arm and guided him back out the door. At first, he resisted, but then he sighed and let Tillinghast bring him out.

"If I live long enough," LeCroix said, "I'm going to kill the bastard myself."

"Who's that?" asked Tillinghast. "Not Colonel Marks."

"No. Kuchner." He'd often had rivals in his work, and how he took care of things then was how he chose to take care of things now. He turned to Tillinghast. "I can find my own way. I have patients to care for. Even if they were my enemy."

19

Tillinghast left him at the end of a lane and LeCroix walked on alone back to the plantation house. The women of the house were gone. Theodolus was gone, too, a bucket of soap and water at the front door. The Union soldiers shrugged when he asked where Theodolus went.

LeCroix took the rest of the day to go up and down the rows, seeing to the men with their infected amputations, finding three dead men in their beds. He told the Union soldiers, who rustled up men to take the bodies away.

It was dark when LeCroix finally sat down at the desk in the surgeon's room. He was exhausted, famished, and frustrated — in that order. Tomorrow he would have to cut away some dead flesh from some men, he knew two men wouldn't last the night, and he needed help. Theodolus had not returned.

He felt something at his shoulder, and he started awake. A woman with a candle stood before him. "Doctor?"

LeCroix rubbed his eyes. "I must have dozed off. Annette, yes?"

She nodded. "Please, come with me. We have a room that the other doctor used."

He followed her into a room on the bottom floor, away enough from the hospital that he could no longer notice the stench. The bed was large and of a feather mattress, looking welcoming to him. But most of all were two small sandwiches on a tray. His mouth watered. He didn't care if they were made of horsemeat; he was ready to eat anything.

"Thank you," he said, and sat down in front of the food.

Annette lit a few candles from hers. "I hope that the cheese is still good," she said.

"It will be fine." He looked around the room. "I appreciate this."

"It's private enough —" LeCroix heard a noise at the door.

Tillinghast appeared in the doorway. "Oh, excuse me," he said. "I heard voices and —"

Annette blushed and said, "I was going to leave." She gave the two men a little bow and nearly fled out of the room.

LeCroix waved Tillinghast in while he fell on the bread and cheese sandwiches. "I haven't eaten all day," he said. The cheese was mostly rind, but he didn't care.

Tillinghast sat across from him. "Is there anything I can do?"

"I need food," he said. "For the men. They were fed once the whole time I was here. And I need a nurse. And I need my slave back."

Tillinghast frowned. "Your slave probably ran away."

"He wouldn't have. He doesn't know where to go."

"There's slaves out in the woods, and beyond. It's only a matter of time before manumission is the law of the land."

LeCroix finished eating his cheese sandwich. "I hope you didn't come here to argue politics with me."

"No," said Tillinghast. "I brought something."

He dipped a hand in his pocket and pulled out a small jar of oil. "I was able to sneak this from the kitchen."

"What if I'm wanted? If someone out there is —"

Tillinghast rose up and kissed LeCroix full on the mouth, his tongue thrust into his mouth. LeCroix leaned back in his chair, moaning loudly, letting Tillinghast push him back with just the kiss.

Both men undressed each other, not slowly, but tugging and pulling on fabric, some which came away in LeCroix' hands, due to the age and use of the clothing.

Naked, they climbed into the bed, and LeCroix began to use the oil on Tillinghast's hole, opening him up slowly, ever so slowly, before replacing his fingers with his hard cock. Tillinghast grabbed a hold of the headboard and pushed against LeCroix, as the two men strained and grunted, trying to remain quiet in case anyone came to the door, Tillingthast shot into the pillow, to avoid getting it all over the bed.

20

And so this continued for three years, through manumission, when LeCroix's slaves disappeared, to never return; when General "Beast" Butler and Captain Mills were replaced, to the end of the war. Tillinghast resigned at the end of the war with the title of Captain, and remained in New Orleans until his death in 1882, two years after the death of his lover, David LeCroix.

SCORPIO

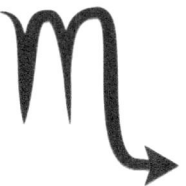

JUNE 30, 1972
ST. LOUIS, MISSOURI

I

My Angel walked into The Garden.

He was head to toe in leather, from the black leather policeman's cap, to the thick black leather boots tied with silver laces that caught the light of the dance floor and glittered. Leather pants hugged his tight and taut figure, his perfectly rounded ass and muscular thighs. He wore a black leather vest with chains in strategic places that jingled a little when he shrugged his massive shoulders. His chest, hairy and thick, poked out from the vest. He had tattoos, like a merchant marine: mermaids and tridents, the Navy crest on one forearm.

I noticed all this because he came within a foot of me. I was at the bar, with two other friends from the district, and all three of us stared unabashedly at this man in leather.

"Two shots of Jack in one glass,"

He had a voice that was deep and resonant, like the voiceover of a movie. He then took his glass and turned to look at us.

Now, we were nothing special to look at. At least I had some definition to my body, while my other two friends were too skinny due to the drugs they used on weekends and some weeknights, like tonight. I didn't touch the stuff, preferring the drug of alcohol to the harder shit like heroin or LSD. Needles scared me, and pills were hard to swallow. Liquid gold was easier.

I wasn't feeling tipsy by this point, but I was feeling emboldened. I said to him, "Hello."

My other two friends giggled and blushed and acted like fifteen-year-old schoolgirls. I ignored them.

"Hello," he said in that voice that I wanted to hear read the phone book, just to keep him talking.

"I've never seen you in here."

"Just got into town," he said, knocking back the drink in one bolt.

Impressive, I thought.

"This place wasn't here the last time I came through."

"When was that?"

"A few years ago."

Some drag queen came over and said, "Heya, big boy."

She had the usual curly blond hair and heavily made up face, too girly for me. She wore heels that were at least six inches high and platform shoes that glittered.

The biker seemed to ignore her.

"It's getting too crowded in here," he said.

He got up from the bar and looked pointedly at me, expecting me to follow. I did dutifully, like a puppet on a string.

Near the bathroom I could hear men moaning, coaxing, and my cock started to get hard. I knew what he was going for, as soon as he pushed me against the wall in the bathroom. He didn't even bother to kiss me. He had a grin on his face, a "Now I've gotcha!" type of smile that made me grin right back at him.

"Good," he said, and cupped my cock roughly through my pants. He squeezed, and I thrust against his hand. "Very good."

A stall became available, and he dragged me into it. The two other guys watched with knowing smiles as he slammed shut the door and didn't bother to even lock it.

He threw me face-forward against the door and undid my pants from behind. He pressed his cool leather pants against my bare ass, and I could feel the muscle straining in there.

"You want this?"

"Fuck yes," I said.

He ground his monstrous meat against my ass. I will admit; I had never done this on the first date, without even knowing the guy's name. But something made me want to worship him, to do whatever he asked or demanded of me.

I heard him unzip something. I got even harder and started to leak. He held my hands up on the door with one hand and I felt his head search out my ass hole.

"Wait, man, wait," I said. He was going to fuck me?

"Wait for what?" he said, his head pressing against my puckered hole.

I felt something warm and wet there — man, he leaked a lot, I thought, and then the next thing I knew, he was inside me.

I screamed. It was bigger than I'd ever had before, and firm, unyielding. He slammed into me, hard enough to rattle the door, and deep enough to hit my guts. He kept holding my hands up and kept pounding into me. I relaxed, taking him, grunting against him, wanting him to at least touch my cock to release it, because it was so hard.

Then he grunted, slamming into me one more time, and I felt the wetness flow in and out of me, down my leg as he seemed to cum in buckets inside me.

He let me go, and peeled me off the door. He shoved me between the toilet and the wall and he stuffed his monster cock into his leather pants. I was still hard, of course, and looked at him, pleading.

He looked down at me, ran a finger down the underside of my cock, making me moan.

"Come back here tomorrow night," he ordered.

He threw open the door and left me there.

I swear, I was so discombobulated, that I couldn't tell what to do. I wanted to bring myself off, but I also wanted him to get me off. I waited. He wasn't going to come back. I knew someone else was waiting for the stall, I pulled myself together, stuffed my softening cock into my pants and left the stall. As I expected, two men were waiting to use it.

"You okay, man?" asked one of my friends when I came out …

No, I wasn't okay. But I needed to see him again. "Where did the guy go?"

"Took someone else outside."

I frowned. Great. Should I come back tomorrow and get used again? Or will he treat me better if I do come back?

2

I didn't know what to think as my friend drove me home that night. My apartment was hot, so I turned on all the fans to try and cool it down, but I was hot too. What was his name? He was in the Navy, that was for certain. Or was he?

I lay down across my bed. It was two in the morning. Luckily, it was the weekend — that's when I usually would go out to bars — and it was July 4th weekend at that.

Would I see him tomorrow night? I needed to get him out of my head if I was going to get any sleep tonight, but my hand had wandered down to my hardening cock. To get him out of my head, I needed to get off.

I took off my pants and shirt. I slept only in my boxers anyway, so this was nothing new. But I pushed aside the waistband and pulled my hard cock out. I went to the nightstand for the lube and a towel, then settled into bed.

It didn't take much — a few strokes before I came in the towel. I kept feeling his touch, when he held my hands up, when he pressed into me, when he plowed through me … yeah, it wasn't much at all.

The next day, Saturday, I had a party to go to in the afternoon. My niece Jackie was turning 16 and they were going to throw a party for her. This meant, of course, I had to deal with my parents and my sister.

My parents didn't know about my lifestyle. My sister suspected but I denied it to her. I knew how they treated my brother when he decided to go out with a Spanish girl — nobody talked to Joey now.

What the hell was I going to get Jackie? I had no idea what kids these days liked. I decided money in a card. I couldn't get something too funny, or too serious — she was 16, after all — and she would be happier with her friends than with her family. I don't know if my brother-in-law was going to spring for a car or not.

Not to mention how firmly Alex, my brother-in-law, was in the closet. I could tell, from the hard-ons he got when he watched football and boxing. He would invite me over for sports parties, and I would pretend to get into it, but I was mostly interested in watching the other guys. He was the only one I noticed with a firm woody each time the camera focused on the players or boxers' sweaty bodies.

One time, during tight quarters in Christmas, he slid next to me and ground his crotch into my ass. At least I could have sworn that, but he when I turned around to look at him, he was looking out the window to the side of him, pretending to not pay attention. I still wonder to this day if that was his first come-on.

They had since moved out of that apartment to a split-level ranch in the outskirts of St. Louis, among other split-level ranches in a suburb development, with postage-stamp sized front lawns, and half-acre back lawns, each with one or two strategically placed trees to create a sense of natural beauty. I drove up to the house, and parked on a side street, walking over to it.

Someone had arrived on a motorcycle, as it was parked in the driveway between two cars. It was a monstrosity of a bike, with big saddlebags, and a huge gas tank on the front, painted a dark blue. The whole bike looked like a construction worker would have to ride it, it was so big.

I examined the bike and walked by it to the front door. It was open, and I could see people through the screen on the other side, in the kitchen, a little ways beyond.

"Hey," I called, when I walked in.

"Hey, yourself," said my sister, Julia.

She waved at me from the kitchen, surrounded by other women who also waved, including my mother, who was stuffing celery sticks with pimento cheese.

I gave Julia a squeeze and a kiss, and kissed my mother, waved to the women.

"Where's Jackie's presents going?"

"Over by the fireplace," said Julia. "The guys are out back hanging around the grill."

I placed my card among a stack of others, and went back into the kitchen. My mother pressed the celery sticks on me.

"Take these outside, will you, John?"

Yes. My family had a thing for names starting with "J." I would say thank the Kennedys for that, but it was a stupid thing on my mother's part. My father got the middle names, so I got the middle name of Patrick. I went by J. P. Miller in most circles, except family.

As I approached the picnic table to place the celery sticks on them, the kids watched me to see if there was anything interesting. Celery sticks were not interesting enough, so they went back to playing. I went over toward the grill.

And I stopped short.

Because standing there, with a bottle of Budweiser in his hand, was my Angel from the Garden.

3

I didn't know what to do exactly. He hadn't seen me yet. His long black hair was tied back in a ponytail. I could see him better in this light; his features were as Romanesque as I remembered: square jaw, strong facial features, blue eyes. Broad shoulders, tapering down to a trim waist, but he wore a t-shirt so I couldn't see his tight abs. And the package, encased in denim this time, was as big as I remembered.

I drew my eyes up to see him looking at me now. Alex turned around from the grill to see me.

"Hey, John."

I needed something to do with my hands. I put them behind my back.

"Hey, Alex."

"Scorp, get the man a beer."

The dark-haired well-built man turned behind him to the bucket of ice and pulled out a bottle. He used the bottle opener on the side of the grill to pop it open and he handed it to me. I thought he gave me a wink, but I wasn't sure.

"John, meet Scorpio, my old pal from college."

I said the usual, "Nice to meet you."

He inclined his head.

"That your motorcycle out there?" I asked, sipping at the beer.

"Yeah," he said in that deep baritone that went right to my bones.

Said one of the other guys, someone I knew from Alex's company, "My wife won't let me get a motorcycle."

Scorpio said, "Fuck the wife."

"I do," he said, with a wolf's grin.

"Obviously not good enough," said another man, "Or she'd let you get the bike."

In the meantime, I was wondering about Scorpio and Alex's arrangement in college. Did Alex know Scorpio went to a gay bar last night, and would have gone tonight if I hadn't shown up? Or was he still going to go? My mind was in a whirlwind of questions and shock. I imagined that Alex and Scorpio both did shit together, exploring, testing each other out.

It took all my willpower not to get my own woody thinking of the two of them in some dorm room together. Alex would definitely be the sub, his short blond hair and white skin spotted with sweat as the two of them went at it in a dorm bed ...

"John?" someone called my name. I don't remember who.

Alex, Scorpio, and the three other guys were looking at me expectantly. "Sorry," I said. "Wool gathering."

"Was talking about the Cardinals. How bad they suck." Scorpio chugged down his beer and tossed the empty into the trash like a pro basketball player making a free throw. It hit with a satisfying crash of glass.

"Aces," said Alex.

I stood around uncomfortably, half-listening to the guys talk baseball, which was not something I was interested in but I could put in a few words here and there to get by. Scorpio drank two more beers then said he had to "drain the vein". As he walked by me, he caught my eye and did wink. I looked down and away.

Thankfully, nobody saw me, or noticed as I left the group to go back into the kitchen. I caught him in the kitchen, talking to the women there, and all of them seemed to want to distance themselves from him. He made no bones about checking out Julia. It's a cliche, but his eyes almost devoured her. She hugged herself and stood in a corner. None of the other women did anything.

"Hey, um, Julia?"

Scorpio turned to me while Julia forced a smile to me. "Yeah?"

"Got any lemonade?"

"Can't handle the beer?" said Scorpio, as he plucked it out of my hand.

"I'm a lightweight," I said.

Scorpio drank it down — it was mostly full — in one long chug. He let out a long "Ahhh," and turned back to me. "Whaddaya press? One-ten?"

"I don't lift weights," I said, as Julia positioned herself away from Scorpio.

"I can see that. Ever thought of trying it?"

"Not really. I'm not into being a muscle-bound brute."

He looked me over, the same way he looked Julia over. He already knew what I looked like from the bottom down, not that he cared. I found myself blushing as he kept staring at me.

"Uh huh," he rumbled, and sneered at Julia as she held out the lemonade to me. 'Toss this out, will ya, honey?" he said, handing her the empty bottle. Then he went further into the house, probably to the bathroom.

Julia shivered. "He gives me the creeps."

"Why invite him over, then?"

"He's Alex's friend. He's staying here for a couple of days, but I've seen how he looks at Jackie. I don't like him."

"Tell Alex," said mom, as she continued to knit. She always knitted something whenever she sat down, everywhere she went.

"Alex is different around him. More ... rude."

Said one of the other women, "They're college buddies. Men always act like that around college buddies. Like they're back in college."

"I can't wait until he's gone."

One of the women, in a long flowing skirt and shirt, who looked more like a hippie than anything, said, "You should tell him how you feel. Clear the air, make things right between you."

I raised an eyebrow. I saw him come down the short hall from the bathroom to the kitchen. He looked between the women, grinned at them, and then at me.

"You still here?"

I held up the lemonade.

"Fuck that shit," said Scorpio, as the women gasped.

My mother snapped, "Watch your language, young man."

He laughed at her. "I'll be outside. With the *men*."

I got the hint and followed him, carrying the lemonade in its fancy glass outside. He led the way back to the grill, which now had kids gathered around it to get the hot dogs and hamburgers right off it. The men had moved to the side under a small elm tree, taking the cooler of beer with them. One of the kids sat down in the chair I was going to take, and gave me a look to dare him to vacate the seat.

"Move," said Scorpio from behind me, but he wasn't talking to me. He was talking to the kid. The kid scampered up and Scorpio hooked the chair, handing it to me. "Fuck the kids, too," he said, heading to where the men gathered, smoking.

Scorpio pounded a pack of Marlboros in his hand, tamping down the tobacco. I took one offered and he lit it for me. I didn't smoke as a rule, because I didn't like how it made me smell — bars were notorious for that. It also dulled the taste buds so that the hamburger would probably taste like ash. Which was fine, since Alex couldn't cook a good burger anyway.

The paper plate was on my lap, but Scorpio didn't even use a plate. Hell, he didn't bother with a napkin, either. He didn't care. "Fuck it all" seemed to be his motto. However, he didn't drip on himself, or make a mess, or care what he looked like while he ate. He still had manners — he didn't talk with his mouth full, and he ate just fine standing up.

He glanced at me at one point, and said, "Hey, when you're done, I wanna show you something."

I ate faster. Brushing crumbs from my lap, I put the paper plate in the trash. He was right behind me. I felt this presence so close to me, and he said, "Come with me."

I followed him to the far back of the yard. Back there was a shed, where Alex kept the grill and lawnmower and other garden implements. It was unlocked, and he opened the door. I had no idea what he planned to show me inside there, since I was familiar enough with the place, so I went inside.

He shut the door and leaned against it. His hand went right to his dick, stroking it through the jeans. "Get on your knees," he ordered me.

It was dusty, dirty, but I didn't care. I got on my knees right in front of him, as he undid his jeans. He pulled out his cock, uncut, mind you, and stroked it right in front of my face. I reached up to touch it.

"Eh eh, don't touch it, except with your mouth."

I licked at the glistening head. The taste was salty-sweet, and drove me wild. I tried to take all of it, and he tried to feed it to me, but I could only get his head and about an inch of the shaft before my gag reflex kicked in and made me pull back.

"How bad you want this?" he asked, as I tried again and again to take more and more. "You want this fucking bad, doncha?"

"Mmmmhmmm," I could only say, my mouth stuffed with cock.

Then I heard someone knock at the door. I froze.

"Who is it?" Scorpio asked casually, as if nothing untoward was going on.

"What're you doing in there, Scorp?" Alex's voice.

I pulled off and started to get up, but Scorpio put a heavy hand on my shoulder keeping me down.

"I'm getting the fuck off." Then he stepped aside and threw open the door. "Wanna join us?"

Alex stared for a long time at Scorpio's cock, wet and hard and sticking straight out. Then he saw me. I looked down sheepishly.

Alex stepped inside and shut the door. "I won't tell if you won't tell," he said to me.

I shook my head. "Take it to my grave."

Alex reached out and stroked Scorpio's cock. He moaned, saying, "Been wanting this since you showed up."

"I know. Now get on your knees and suck me."

Alex groaned and did just that. He didn't get as far down as I did.

"You're out of practice, eating pussy these eight years. You," he said to me, "give him a hand job while he sucks me."

This was a dream come true. I undid and pushed down his shorts and deftly pulled out his cock. It was a whole lot smaller than Scorpio's, but it was something I had wanted to do for years. Alex got bigger in my hand as I stroked him. He moaned loudly, his mouth wrapped around Scorpio's cock.

"This is bullshit, Alex, you need to take lessons." He pulled his cock out of Alex's mouth, and pointed it at me. "This guy, he's a fuckin' pro."

Alex looked disappointed as I released his cock and took Scorpio's instead. I took him in my mouth, not caring that Alex had just slobbered all over it. Scorpio rocked his hips, thrusting further and further into my mouth, inch by inch.

"You got it," Scorpio said, and I felt his cock expand in my mouth. He was going to cum, and I was going to swallow it —

But he pulled his cock out and instead came all over my face. I didn't expect that, but Alex moaned loudly, watching the exchange, and then he too, shot all over the dusty floor.

Meanwhile, I was hard as a rock in my shorts, and I wanted so badly to get off. But in a way, I wanted to savor this, to remember Alex's look of sadness as Scorpio pulled away from him.

Scorpio grinned down at me. "Damn, that was good."

I could hear my sister calling for Alex. "Alex? Jackie's going to open her presents now. Alex?"

Alex swiftly put himself back in his pants, as I found a dusty rag to wipe my face. He waited for Scorpio to slowly stuff that monster cock away. Once he finished that, he opened the door to the shed and stepped outside. Scorpio and I stood in the doorway as Alex went down the rear lawn to the house.

"I'll be seein' you later," Scorpio said to me. "I don't need to watch no little slut open her sixteen year old presents."

"We could stay out here, drink beer," I said.

I wanted to know more about him. What did he go to college for? And why was he now a biker?

He grinned. "Rather drink beer with your mouth on my cock in the bar," he said.

"I'm sure that can be arranged," I said.

He laughed, and headed out to the front yard. I ended up going in the house, watching Jackie open presents.

4

At dusk, I finally bid my farewells to the family. Jackie got her car; a 1962 Nova that had seen better days. My mind was still in the shed, thinking about Alex, surprised at how he just let Scorpio have his way with him. I wasn't surprised that Scorpio held that kind of sway. I was surprised that Alex, a man's man, who wouldn't be caught dead watching some romantic movie even with his wife, dropped to his knees before a bear of a man and did his bidding.

Maybe after Scorpio left, I would be able to do something like this with Alex. Maybe we could have an affair. Maybe Alex would suck me off sometime.

Those thoughts ran through my mind as I found a parking spot near The Garden. I saw a few motorcycles parked out front, and I knew that one of them must be Scorpio's. This was the first time I was going to be walking in there alone. Usually I had two guys I knew from hanging around the water cooler. We would go meet up at Fitzpatrick's for an hour and then leave together to come to The Garden. If my job knew that I frequented The Garden, I'd be out of my job so fast I wouldn't even notice how.

The Garden was crowded. I'd never come in on a Saturday night, and didn't expect it to be this bad. Lesbians and drag queens, butches and leather, were everywhere. I didn't even have room at the bar. I stood in the middle of the floor, confused and overwhelmed with the music, lights and people. This was not my type of scene.

I saw him in the same clothes that he had been in at the party. He was talking to some twink who blushed and giggled at the attention. I felt a fire in my chest. How dare he? He knew I was coming.

I would have liked to knock back a drink for some liquid courage, but instead I strode across the room going right to him. He looked up from the twink to see me, and he turned from him, giving me a broad smile. That eased up on the fire in my chest a little.

Then my brain kicked in. It's not like we were going out with each other. It was sex, right? No strings attached?

"Hey, John," he said, putting his arm around my shoulders. He turned his back on the twink who gave me a dirty look.

"Jay," I said. "Only my family calls me John."

"Why Jay?"

"I don't like John."

He looked down at my hands. "Buy you a drink?"

"Sure."

"Lemonade?" he asked with a grin.

"Since you're buying, make it a Manhattan."

He chuckled and fought his way through a bar, ordering a Manhattan for me and a shot for himself. We walked over to a corner table that was immediately vacated by two drag queens. I sipped my drink — it was powerful strong.

"Your family's fucked up, man," he said.

"Whose isn't these days?"

"Alex, man, we used to have a fuckin' blast in college. Now he's all," he waved his hand. "Fuckin' pussy-whipped."

"That's what happens," I said.

"It ain't happening to you. Or me."

"Not yet. My mother's getting worried, though."

He chuckled. "Fuck them."

"Easier said than done. You know what happened to my other brother, Joey?"

He drank his shot. "Don't care. Care about yourself, man. Fuck everyone else."

I sipped my drink. I wished I could be like him. No, I had to work in sales in a bank. I would love to take a ride with him on a bike, abandon everything, and live on the road ... with him.

"What about friends? Relationships?"

He drank his shot. "Alex is one."

"You must've had some really good relationship with him before in college."

He grinned. "Yeah. But now." The grin faded. "His fucking wife's got him by the balls."

I sipped the drink. It was too strong for me, so I put it down and pushed it away. He took it from me, sniffed it before drinking some.

"His wife happens to be my sister," I said.

"She doesn't have you by the balls."

"No." She never really did.

He drank more of the Manhattan, barely hiding a disgusted look. "I meant what I said."

"Meant what?"

"That you're a fuckin' pro at sucking cock."

I know I blushed; I felt the heat rise to my face.

"You're a good fuck, too. Whaddaya say we get outta here and go somewhere else?"

"Somewhere else? Like where?"

"Your place, maybe?"

I wasn't about to bring this guy to my place. Not only would the neighbors talk, but I didn't know what he'd steal from me.

"Don't trust me?"

I didn't know how to answer that. "Do you want me to be honest?"

"That could be a start."

"My neighbors are nosy."

I knew he was going to say when he said. "Fuck the neighbors."

I laughed. "No thanks, they're too old."

I happened to look up to see the twink heading in our direction. He made a beeline for Scorpio but was talking to me.

"Hey," he said. "I was talking to him."

Scorpio raised his head. "You know of any hotels?"

The kid's look brightened. "There's the Easton."

The Easton was a fleabag of a motel just south of here. I was hoping for something a little more ... tasteful.

"They rent by the hour?" Scorpio asked.

"Yeah. They rent to anyone."

Scorpio got up. "Let's go." The twink started to follow, but Scorpio put a hand out and said, "Not you."

"What?" I think he was going to cry.

"You're not invited."

"But —"

Scorpio turned to me. "I'll follow you."

The twink didn't move from the middle of the floor where we left him. I kind of felt sorry for him. Kind of.

5

We arrived together at the hotel. I had never been here, but I'd heard things. It wasn't my type of place, but Scorpio didn't seem to mind it as he went inside the office. I wasn't sure what to do, so I stayed outside.

He seemed to be taking a long time, and I got out of the car, but he came out as I shut the door. He held something up and beckoned me. I followed him, as he looked at what he had in his hand and each of the doors.

He stopped at door number 117 and put the key he had in his hand in the lock. He turned the handle and opened the door. It was hot, and the heat escaped out to us like a wave. It smelled like mold.

"Oh, great," I muttered.

He walked in, and I hoped the roaches scattered.

"There's still your place."

I shook my head as I put the light on. The room had a caving-in bed, two chairs from the '40's, a plastic table, and a lamp. There was a bathroom that I didn't need at the moment.

Scorpio closed the curtains and switched on the air conditioner. It stank of dust.

"How long do we have here?" I asked.

"Two hours."

"That's it?"

"How long do you want to spend here?"

"Okay, I see your point."

He turned to me, cupped the back of my head, and pulled me in for a bruising kiss. I shoved off his vest, the chains rattling when they hit the bed. He peeled off my t-shirt, and roughly groped my pecs.

"Nice," he said.

I moaned, and got his shirt off. I moved my head to his hairy chest, and looked at the tattoos. I licked the scorpion's tail near his nipple, then his nipple.

"Fuck, yeah," he said. "Suck my tits, man."

I was swollen in my shorts and wanted so badly to get off, considering I hadn't in the shed. I worked on his nipples, flicking them with my tongue, biting lightly, getting a hiss out of him. I sucked on the other nipple, which had some sort of tribal tattoo around it. He pushed me away, pushed me toward the bed. "Lay down, on your stomach."

I did what he said, and he moved behind me. I couldn't see what he was doing, but he stripped me of my shorts. My cock rubbed against the rough coverlet of the bedspread. Scorpio took one of my arms and lifted it up.

He put a handcuff on the post of the bed, and then around my right wrist.

"Hey!"

He grabbed my other hand and tied a chain around my wrist. I struggled, but he was stronger, and he chained my other hand to the post.

"Trust me," he said.

"Fuck you, pal. Untie me!"

He whipped something across my back, It was light, but bit into my back. It wasn't a chain. It might have been leather.

"What's the safe word?" he asked, and whipped me again.

"How the fuck should I know?"

He whipped me again.

I cried out, "Pomegranate!"

"Wrong!"

He flogged me. Over and over, and I would yell random words. No one came in to stop him. No one banged on the wall. I was the only one yelling, getting whipped, until finally I just grunted whenever the lash came down. My back felt hot and I knew I was bleeding. Tears flowed freely.

"Please stop," I whimpered.

I had come, without even realizing it. He stopped, and I felt him lick my back. It hurt, it burned, I cried.

He undid the chain around my wrist. I kept my hand up there anyway — what was I going to do? He stretched across my back and unlocked the handcuff around my other wrist. He lay on top of me, his cooler body across my burning back, and he held me tenderly, and stroked my body and my member. I wanted to turn around in his arms and punch him in the face.

But my body betrayed me as I felt his wet cock search out the crack of my ass, find the puckered soft spot of my hole. He leaked so much, he only had to push forward and his head was inside me.

He thrust even further, and I groaned loudly, and he rose from my back. The cool air hit the hot skin of my back, and again, his hot tongue licked my wounds. This time, I felt my body stiffen and tense, and I came again in his hand, my climax tightening my ass around him, as he continued to thrust relentlessly into me. He released my cock, and used his hands as leverage as he pounded me into the bed, slamming the bed into the wall with every thrust.

Then he grunted, and I felt his hot cream coat my insides. I intentionally tightened my ass to milk him as he spasmed inside me. He collapsed on top of me, absently stroking my arms and pulling my arms down, hugging me.

"You asshole," I said finally.

He chuckled.

It took all of my willpower — the same willpower that made me advance to see him in the bar — to pull away and disengage. I stood up. I hoped I looked angry; at least I tried to.

He was grinning, like a cat that had the canary.

That pissed me off even more as I went around the bed to get my clothes.

"So soon?" he said.

I hissed in pain as I pulled my shirt on. I didn't dare look in the mirror in the hotel. I'd look back at home to assess the damage. I just glared at him.

Some angel, I thought.

He sat up once he saw me grab my keys and head to the door. "John —"

I walked out on the angel of my dreams.

6

I was so sore, I couldn't lie down. Not for the first time, was I glad that I had an extra day off to recover. July

4th was Tuesday, and I only had to work tomorrow. I didn't know if I was going to make it.

It was noon before I finally got out of bed, to see the sheets were stained red in places. My back itched like crazy. I couldn't see in my mirror at home how bad it looked. How many wounds had he caused with that whip?

At one, the landlord would be stopping by for his rent. I got out that envelope and bustled around the kitchen, cleaning up. I heard the knock on the door at a little before one. I picked up the envelope and answered the door.

"Hi, Mr. —," I said, before registering who it was.

Scorpio stood there, in a white wife-beater shirt and jeans. I could see his tattoos clearly now.

"You gonna invite me in?" he said.

"How did you know where I lived?"

"I looked it up in the address book at Alex's house." He invited himself in. He looked around. "Nice place. I think they call it 'cozy'."

What would the neighbors say about the bike outside? Would they believe I invited him in for a game of chess? He just walked into my house, as if he was looking at it to rent, and went into my living area.

Another knock on the door, and I answered it, this time looking to see who it was. "Mr. Langley," I said, and thrust the envelope out at him.

"Hi, Jay. Everything all right?"

Did I look nervous?

"I have a guest."

"Oh, all right." He finished writing out the receipt and gave it to me. He never counted the money in front of me, because he trusted me. "Have a good week."

"Thanks, you too."

I closed the door on his back, and went to the living area. Scorpio had plopped himself on my couch and was looking at the magazines on my coffee table. "Better Homes and Gardens?" he said, dropping it on the table. "It's like a doctor's office."

"I wanted some ideas to brighten my kitchen. Now what do you want?"

He grinned. "What do you think I want?"

"Is that all you live for? Sex?"

"Lemme ask you this, then, what do *you* want?"

What did I want? A normal relationship, like men and women could share, except it would be with a man? Did I want a romantic relationship? Did I want a man like Scorpio in my life, a possible destructive force with a "Fuck 'em all" mentality — probably someone would would fuck me over too if he got tired of me? Did I want that? Was I going to get that with him?

"I don't know," I said. I didn't.

"You don't trust me."

"After last night, who would?"

"You think I went too far?"

"I wanted you to stop."

"But I didn't really hurt you."

"You fucking scared the shit out of me."

He raised his left eyebrow. "I made you a stronger man because of it."

"Pain doesn't make you stronger," I said.

"But it doesn't make you weak, either."

I threw my hands up in the air. "The hell with this."

"Look. I'm sorry if I scared you. I won't do that shit again." He leaned back, the tattoos catching the light. All of them were of sea scenes; fish, mermaids, coral and kelp instead of roses and thorns. "Though you got off."

It was true I had gotten off like I never did before. But I didn't want him to think that I enjoyed it. Maybe I did. Part of me did. But part of me, the more rational one, was scared to death.

"Lemme see your back."

I peeled off my t-shirt and turned around for him. "You're healing okay," he said. "Got any peroxide?"

"Yeah," I said, and went to the bathroom. I came out and he stood there in the doorway, holding his hand out for the brown bottle. He poured some of the cool hydrogen peroxide on the wounds of my back, tenderly patting them with a dry facecloth.

"You'll have scars," he said. "Something to tell your grandkids."

I snorted.

"You haven't told your family, I reckon."

"No. Not after what they did to my brother, I don't think I should."

"What did they do?"

He finished patting me down and stepped away. Again, he stood in the doorway.

"He's going out with some Spanish girl. They don't talk to him anymore."

"That's fuckin' stupid."

"They don't talk to my dad, either." I turned around to look at him.

"Why not?"

I shrugged. "My mom, I guess. She raised us alone." I out on my t-shirt. "And you're doing it again."

"Doing what?"

"Finding out all about me and I don't know anything about you."

"All right," he said and backed out of the bathroom while I walked forward into my kitchen. "I'm immortal."

I stared at him, then burst out laughing. "You're kidding, right?"

"No," he said. "I've only told three people in my life that."

"And then you had to kill them?"

"Want me to?"

"No, I mean, Jesus, no ... Christ, you're serious."

"Very serious. Want me to prove it?" He tucked a hand in his front pocket and took out a switchblade.

"No," I said, but he already sliced his palm open. He made no noise, the blood welled up and he squeezed his hand, letting the blood drip onto the floor. "Aw, man, don't —"

He held out his hand. Blood was all over his palm, but even I could see the wound was gone. He went to the sink and washed his hands, getting a bit of paper towel to wipe the blood from the floor.

I just stood there, watching him clean up the mess. He squatted down and looked up at me. He was eye-level with my crotch. He leaned forward, and mouthed my cock through the shorts I wore. I gasped; I suspected he was distracting me.

"Why ... three?"

"Three what?"

"Three people?"

"Because I loved them." He straightened up. "They died." He looked into my eyes. It was like looking into a maelstrom, so intense was his gaze. "You don't love me," he said.

"I don't know you."

"You don't love me, because I wouldn't have healed if you did."

I blinked. "What do you mean?"

He said, "I'm immortal until I meet someone who loves me as much as I love them."

"Wait. Are you saying —"

He looked around the apartment. "This place is big enough for two."

I backed up, into the wall, my hands up in surrender. "Wait a second. Hold on, whoa, whoa, whoa." I knew what he was trying to say.

"I have six degrees, one from Harvard, another from Princeton," he said. "I worked on the Manhattan Project. I worked for Pinkerton, Wells Fargo, and I was the sheriff of Norton, Colorado for thirty years. I've been in the Navy and the Marines, and the Canadian Mounties. Now you know all about me."

I needed to sit down to take this all in. *Manhattan Project? Pinkerton?* "How ... how old are you?"

"Old enough to remember Shakespeare's first performance of *As You Like It*."

I walked past him to the kitchen table, and sat down. "You're five hundred years old?"

He shrugged. "Lost count."

"What's your real name?"

"The name I was born with or the name I have now?"

"Both."

"George Miller. I'm Arthur Kenneth Miller right now." He smiled. "Do I look like an Artie to you?"

He had the same last name as me. That should have been a red flag, but it wasn't.

"That doesn't matter."

"Good, cuz I hate being called Artie."

I put my head in my hands. "I still don't know much about you."

"How about we get to know each other, then?"

I looked up at him. If a man like him could beg, he would have. I didn't expect the intense look in his eyes, the pleading in his face. I had never thought of having a serious relationship with anyone. This was something dropped from the heavens.

What was I going to say? No?

"All right," I said, not knowing that would be the most tumultuous thing I would ever admit.

He stood over me and took off his shirt. I studied the dark green ink of his tattoos, except the scorpion over his heart, which was red. It was out of place in the sea of tattoos, but it mystified me. I kissed it, and he pulled away.

"Let me make it up to you," he said, and dropped to his knees. He pushed open my legs and again mouthed my cock through my shorts. His hot breath caused me to groan and lean forward. He used his teeth to pull down my shorts, exposing my leaking cock.

He licked me from base to tip, his tongue flicking the head and crown. If he was immortal, he must have done this kind of thing before, and probably knew all kinds of different sexual methods to bring me to climax. The whipping was just a start to the unusual things he could probably do to make me cum.

Man, I wanted that, and I moaned even louder as he professionally took me down. He took me all the way down, his nose in my pubes, his tongue at the base of my balls, as he started to suck me, his head moving up and down on me.

Oh, God, he knew what he was doing. This was a hundred times better than getting head in the back of The Garden. I was lost in the feelings that he was giving me, my body tensing and my hand entwined in his short black hair.

"Scorpio ... I'm going to ..."

He paused, flicking his tongue across my head, dipping a tip into my slit, and I lost it. He put his mouth around my cock and sucked and swallowed my jism, grunting as I continued to shoot seemingly over and over into him.

I slumped in my chair, as he rose, then he kissed me, a tender kiss that I could taste myself on him. I put my arms around him and held him for a moment before he rose to his full height.

He was hard in his jeans, and I knew now it was my turn.

7

I exited my car into the heat of the summer, and walked to the bank's main doors. Already my shirt was sticking to my back, and I could swear that people could see through my shirt to see the wounds on my back. I carried my jacket over my arm, along with my briefcase.

I didn't expect to worry too much about my day, as most people were out because of the holiday tomorrow. I showed my badge to the security guard who nodded and buzzed me through the doors to the employee elevators. I saw Frank, one of the guys from the Friday night bar at Fitzpatrick's (not The Garden) and nodded to him.

Someone slapped me on the back and I winced as that person said, "Jay! How was your weekend?"

It was Leo, one of the managers, but not of my department. "Fine," I said. "Yours?"

"Great!"

We both climbed onto the elevator. This elevator was slow and clunky, and sometimes stopped a half-inch below the floor, but it got us where we were going, in general.

"You're looking good."

"Thanks." Though I felt exhausted.

"How's your new manager? What's his name?"

"Dion? He's okay, I guess."

"Just okay?"

I didn't want to tell him that three people were looking for other jobs in the company because they hated Dion. I just shut up, did my work, made my quota every month, and didn't rock the boat. Because of that, Dion didn't notice me.

"So far," I said. "He's still getting to know us."

"Taking his own sweet time over it," Leo said.

The elevator stopped at my floor, and I said, "'scuse me," while I left. Leo waved when the door closed.

I went to my desk, across from a kid I called Dopey. He hardly ever came in on Mondays, because he was so stoned when he did come in. He chain-smoked and I found myself smoking with him. I only smoked at work. It kept me awake.

Next to me, Eddie came in, and, on the other side of me, was Red. They talked about their wives and kids, and I sat and listened, until the phone banks lit up and it was time to sell, sell, sell.

But all I could think about was Scorpio. How, without coming out and saying it, he said he loved me. Not that I didn't love him; I just didn't trust him, not after the hotel.

My brain resolved that he would have to earn that trust for me to love him, like I almost did when I first met him.

Did I love him at one point? He was good in bed, that was certain, but a little too kinky for me. Would he next put a ball gag in my mouth, dress me in leathers and have me worship him?

Okay, that didn't sound like a bad idea.

What the hell was I thinking? I left work, having not made my quota since I was so involved in thinking about Scorpio. It was a good thing I had tomorrow off. Taking back roads to avoid the traffic, I ended up at home in an hour. I didn't want to go to the grocery store today though I should have gone this weekend. I think I had a couple of packages of hamburger left so I could make some American Chop Suey sans onions and peppers for dinner.

I climbed the stairs to my apartment and opened the door. Dropping my briefcase at the door, I turned to look at my kitchen table.

A dozen roses, in a crystal vase, sat on the kitchen table.

8

Those roses weren't there this morning when I left, and I had locked the door when I left for work. I cautiously walked into my apartment, half expecting to see someone rifling through my underwear drawer looking for my budget envelopes. Nothing seemed gone. Not my jewelry box, that I got at an estate sale with my very few cuff links, and my high school class ring. My living room didn't look tossed.

I stood in the doorway between my living room and the kitchen when I heard the rumble of a motorcycle. I went to the living room window and looked out to see Scorpio dismounting from his motorcycle right in front of the house.

I walked over to my door and threw it open so I could see him come up the stairs. I put on my most angry face, so that when he looked up at me as he climbed the stairs, he would see I was not in the least bit happy.

"Hey," he said with a smile, even though I could have sworn I looked angry. He ignored it.

"Did you break into my house?"

"I didn't break in. I let myself in. You know, first time guest, second time family?" He stood very close to me. "Do you like them?"

My body reacted in a way I didn't want to. We stood close enough to kiss. But not in the hallway.

I stepped aside, and he walked in. As soon as I shut the door, though, he did kiss me, a long, deep, sensual kiss that my body hungered for.

His tongue lingered on my lip for a moment before he asked again, "Do you like them?"

"They're beautiful, yes, but you didn't have to break into my house."

"What was I going to do, leave them at the door? You said you have nosy neighbors."

"Nobody saw you come in?"

"Nobody saw me come in," he reassured me, as he kissed me again. I found my body arching into his embrace, "Though your cough medicine expired."

I tensed. "You went in my medicine cabinet?"

"And looked at the books on your shelf yesterday. That shows me what a person really is."

I separated myself from him and went into my kitchen. He followed. "Want a pizza for dinner?"

"No, I have food." I pulled out a box of elbows and some hamburger from the freezer.

"Are you going over Alex's tomorrow?"

"No, why?"

"They're having a pool party."

"I wasn't invited."

"Crash it."

"I don't fuck off my family," I said, starting a fire under the frying pan to get the hamburger defrosted. I wondered why I wasn't invited to their Fourth of July pool party. Was it something I said or did at Jackie's?

I kept looking at the roses on my kitchen table more than I looked at Scorpio. Finally, I went and smelled them.

He smiled. "You do like them."

My phone rang. Leaving the meat to cook on the stove, I answered the phone.

"Hello?"

"John," said Julia, my sister. "I'm so sorry to call you so late. We're having a cookout tomorrow. Want to come?"

I looked at Scorpio, who had taken out his switchblade and was balancing the tip on his finger. Coincidence?

"Sure," I said. "Want me to bring anything?"

"Just yourself," she said.

"I can do that."

"Great. See you at noon."

I hung up and looked at Scorpio. He whistled tunelessly. "Did you?"

"Did I what?"

"I don't know, say something? Do something?"

He flicked the switchblade closed. "You care too much about what other people think. What would you want to be if you didn't have to worry about what other people thought?"

"In a way, I want to be like you."

He grinned. "That's what I thought."

"But you keep saying 'Fuck 'em all' and I just can't do that."

"I've lived too long to care."

"If I do love you," I said, and I got a little fire in my chest when I spoke those words, "Do I become immortal?"

"No," he said. "I will die with you. But our souls live forever as one. The goddess promised that."

"The goddess? What goddess?"

"Ishtar."

"Never heard of her."

"She's a goddess of love and war. We brothers — six to start, then twelve for each of the zodiac — she claims us from Erishkigal the goddess of the underworld and gives us life."

"What are you supposed to do?"

"Help humanity."

"So why aren't you out there ... I don't know, stopping them from destroying the Amazon or something?"

"We help one person at a time. Or sometimes ourselves." He nodded to the frying pan. "Your burger."

I broke it apart in the frying pan, asking him questions. "What do you mean yourselves?"

"Because she's the goddess of love and war, we're always looking for love and we are always warriors. I fought in the Revolution, the Civil War, and both world wars. Sometimes I met my brothers on the battlefield as friends, sometimes enemies. If we help someone at the same time, because we love them, then that's all the better."

"You must fall in love a lot."

"Only twice before."

I nodded, and reached for the bottle of Ragu. I put the elbows in some boiling water.

"I interviewed for a job," he said.

I turned around to look at him. "You did?"

"At The Garden. As a bartender."

"Did you get it?"

"I start Thursday." He grinned. "See? I told you I could get a job easy."

"So that means you're sticking around."

"With you."

"Scorpio —"

He got up from the table and hugged me. "Please, I'm asking you."

I looked beyond his shoulders to the roses. He was trying. He could — and would — change. For me.

I turned around in his arms, dangerously close to the stove. "Let me finish cooking this?"

He moved his hands down my chest to my groin, and paused there, pressing his palm against my cock. Of course it sprang to life. He nuzzled into my neck, kissing the back of my neck as his fingers traced the outline of my cock through my pants.

"Scorpio, please, let me finish this."

"You can finish it," he said into my ear. "Let me have a little fun, too."

I poured the sauce into the frying pan and stirred it while he continued to get me hard in my pants. He didn't take me out, but instead I tented the cotton pleated pants that I wore. He licked and kissed, nibbled and sucked, and

I tried so hard not to turn around in his arms and beg him to take me right then and there.

The elbows were ready, so I removed them from the stove. I got the colander, having to bend down under the sink to get it. He rubbed my ass as I came up, and he squeezed it. I poured the hot elbows into the colander, and he stepped away, letting me get the hot sauce into the pan, mix it with the elbows and got two plates.

He practically poured pepper onto his dinner. My dick had finally calmed down as I ate. When we finished, he cleaned up. He had taken off his vest because of the heat, and I watched his back muscles as he washed dishes, watching the tattoos of a pair of torn bat wings on his back bunch and flex.

I usually watched TV after dinner, so I went into the living room. He came with me. I switched on ABC and we sat on my couch, settling in for some comfortable cuddling. He held me and kissed me, slowly bringing me to a boil.

I didn't get to see the Monday Night Movie.

9

The next morning, he woke me up by giving me a squeeze in bed. "Happy Fourth."

I snapped my eyes open. Oh, shit. I turned my body to face him. "You're still here."

"Yes? And?"

"I thought you were going to leave."

"You looked too beautiful lying there asleep. I wanted to stay."

The neighbors. My sister. Dear God.

But I'm glad he didn't leave.

"I'll make some pancakes," he said, and rolled out of bed.

He was naked. As was I. I hadn't slept naked with a man. Ever. He pulled on his boxers and went to the kitchen. I blinked sleep out of my eyes, and went to the bathroom, the "Oh, shit" thinking slowly finding its way out of my head.

Did my neighbors even care?

I put on my shorts and went into the kitchen. He was spooning out silver dollar pancakes in my large frying pan. "You got something against bacon?"

"No, why?"

"Should have bacon with pancakes."

"I haven't gone shopping."

He made a *tsk*-ing noise.

"I've been busy. And all the stores are going to be closed today."

"I suppose that's a good enough excuse." He found the spatula in the drawer and flipped the pancakes one at a time. "What about syrup?"

"Yeah, I got that." I found it in the back of my fridge.

Watching a tattooed badass biker cook made me smile at the irony. I don't know why, what made me do it, but I hugged him. He chuckled and squeezed my arms with his hands.

"We've got until noon," he said. "After this, want to take a shower?"

"Together?"

"Sure. Conserve the hot water."

"We can't have sex in the shower," I said. "The hot water won't last that long."

"Oh, it will," he said, and kissed me.

10

After pancakes, I brought him into my bathroom. There wasn't much to it — a claw-and-ball bottomed bathtub with a curtain around it; a shower added as an afterthought inside it. The window let in the summer light, facing the east. I stripped from my clothes, and he stripped as well. I pushed aside the curtain, bent over and turned on the water.

If I wanted a luxurious bath, this would be the bathtub for it, but as a shower, I had to be careful not to slip.

"Be careful," I said, stepping into the bathtub.

He looked down as he entered the bathtub. "You need one of those rubber mats they use on bathtubs to not slip."

"I know," I said. "I keep forgetting."

I closed the curtain and he looked around, grinning. "I can fuck you in here," he said. He then sat down in the bathtub. It started to fill up with water.

I stood and watched him, as he beckoned. There was plenty of room for me to kneel above him, and I did. He took a hold of both of our cocks with one hand and stroked them, as the hot water from the shower beat on my already abused back.

I don't know how the bathtub started filling up because I didn't put a stopper on the drain. He reached over behind me and shut off the water when the water came up to his chest. He found the soap, and then he tenderly lathered me up with it, his hands all over me. I moaned and rubbed my cock against his.

The water was warm as he pulled me forward, again aiming his cock against my hole. He pushed my hips downward, and I felt him spear me. I had never been in this position before, and I didn't have the strength in my legs to raise and lower myself on him. So I just sat there for a long moment, savoring him inside me.

Then the water surrounded me and seem to lift me up, buoyed on its surface, and his cock just barely came out of me. Then I was heavier than the water again, and I came crashing down with a grunt.

The water lifted me again, and I looked around. "How?"

"This is my element," he said, and I came down again.

Over and over, the water lifted me and let me down. He started to stroke me in the water, and I felt him suddenly stiffen, his body tense.

"Gods, yes," he moaned, and I came back down on him as he threw his head back and exhaled sharply. "Oh, fuck, yeah ..."

I felt the warmth spread inside me. He jerked my cock, but I wasn't ready. I was too distracted by the water lifting me and dropping me than to really pay attention to what he was doing to me. He released me and looked at me. The water started to go down the drain.

"What's wrong?"

"Your element?"

He lifted his hands, letting the water pass through them. "Water is my element."

"You have control over water?"

"Me and two of my brothers."

I got off of him. "You need to tell me what the hell is going on."

He put a hand on my chest. "Do you love me?"

I turned away from him as I climbed out of the bathtub. I didn't want him to see my shocked look. "What does that have to do with anything?"

"I'm immortal only until someone loves me as much as I love him."

"How can you love me?" I said, standing there naked and dripping wet. "You don't even know me."

"I know your soul." He sat up in the bathtub and also climbed out. "Get dressed and I'll tell you everything."

He got dressed in the same clothes he had on yesterday except he was barefoot as we went into the living room. The shades were down to keep the sunlight from beating down in the room, but it was still hot. I put on the fans.

He sat down on the couch and held his arms out to me. I sighed and sat down next to him, and he pulled me close to him.

He began, "Every so often, the Lady Ishtar searches for twelve warriors in the underworld to do her bidding in the world."

"Ishtar?"

"Goddess of love and war from the Babylonians."

"But why?"

"She wants to help humanity in some fashion. Or it's to amuse her. None of us know."

"Us."

"My eleven brothers. Men with powers of the Zodiac. I'm Scorpio." He chuckled. "Obvious, right?"

"You mean there's one for each of the signs?"

"Yes. I've met them, at least the ones alive."

"They're not all alive?"

"Remember when I said that I'm immortal only until someone loves me like I love them? That's our curse, I guess you could say; when we've lived out our lives, the Lady Ishtar sends our soulmate for us to find in the world, and then we die together."

"So after you, there's no more Scorpio?"

"I'm the third with that name," he said. "There will be others after me. There are always twelve of us brothers alive, but they could be different ones.The man who is Taurus now is not the same man who was Taurus with the Babylonians."

"And you're all Babylonian warriors?"

"I was from Wales. I haven't lived as long as some of my other brothers. I think Aquarius is the longest lived."

"I'm an Aquarius," I said.

"No wonder we get along," he said with a grin.

I smiled and snuggled a little closer to him. My back didn't hurt as much anymore. The whipping was only a memory. "Okay, so you each have powers that belong to the zodiac. What's your power?"

"Let's not get into that."

I turned around to face him. "Tell me."

He looked at my eyes. "Death and resurrection."

I know I leaned back a little. "What?"

He looked down. "I can control death."

"That's ... that's ..." I don't know what that was. I wanted to break out into a grin and say *"Amazing"*, but I wasn't sure how he'd take it. But then I thought about it. "You can kill people?"

"And bring them back to life."

"Like zombies?"

"No. Like pull their souls back to their bodies so they can live a little longer. But death will always claim them. I've done it often enough, and no matter what, they die at the end." I touched his chest. He put his hand on top of mine. "Can we talk about something else?" He looked back at me.

"Why do we get along?" I asked.

"You're an air sign. Air and water usually get along." He hugged me. "Is that enough for you now?"

Oh, I knew I'd have questions galore. But I was satisfied with being in his arms. I kissed him and lay my head on his chest.

II

So we were fashionably late, about 12:30, arriving together. Less cars were parked around the house this time around, so I got a good spot right in front of the house. Scorpio parked between the cars in the driveway again, negotiating his big bike between them.

He opened the door and walked in, holding the door open for me. No one was in the kitchen; it was too hot in the house. Everyone was outside, my mother, sister and ... my brother, Joey. Alone.

"Hey," I said, grinning from ear to ear and walking up to Joey. He gave me a cocky smile and we hugged each other. "How are you? How've you been?"

"Good, okay. How are you doing?" He looked up at Scorpio, who stood off to the side, his thumbs hooked around the loop of his jeans, looking tempting. "Who's that?"

"Alex's friend from college," I said. "He pulled in when I did."

"Oh," said Joey. Scorpio was watching me like a hawk, though. "So, how are you?"

"Okay. Where is everybody?"

"In the pool. I didn't bring a suit."

"Don't need a suit," said Scorpio.

Joey said, "Well, I can't go in naked."

Scorpio shrugged. "I'm sure it's nothing nobody's seen before."

Joey put his arm around me and pulled me to the side, walking toward the rear of the yard where the pool was. "John," he said. "Are you ..."

I know I either went pale or blushed; I couldn't tell. I stopped walking and stood in the middle of the yard. Was it that obvious, in the way Scorpio was looking at me?

"Hey," yelled Julia from the pool. My mom was in there too, and so was Alex and Jackie. "Did you bring your suit?"

"It's in the car," I said. Of course, it was there from the last time I had gotten in their pool about two weeks ago. It should be dry by now.

"I'll go with you," said Joey. We walked around the house instead of through it. Scorpio was gone.

"Where's your girlfriend?"

"We broke up," Joey said when we got to my car. I opened the trunk and took out the pair of swimming trunks. Yep, they were dry.

"I'm sorry to hear that."

He shrugged. "It wouldn't have worked out. I did learn some Spanish, though."

"That's positive."

"You and that guy ..."

"We happened to arrive at the same time," I said, lying through my teeth.

"Look," he said and leaned close to me. "I broke up because I couldn't take not being able to talk to anyone. Mom wouldn't answer the phone. Julia kept telling me it was because of Anita. I know how it feels to be kept on the outside, John."

"What are you trying to say?"

He looked at the ground. "John, it wouldn't surprise me if you were a gay. But I don't care what mom or Julia would do. I'd still be your brother."

"It wouldn't surprise you? What the hell does that mean?"

"You've been a bachelor for way too long. You brought home that one girl in high school — and that's it. You're 28, for Pete's sake. You should have at least a girlfriend."

"Could it be I haven't found the right girl?"

"John, man. You don't have to lie to me."

I slammed shut the trunk. "It wouldn't surprise you, huh? You think I'm one of those limp-wristed little feminine queers?"

"Well, no."

"Then be surprised, because I'm not." Which was the truth. I thrust the swimming trunks at him. "Here, have a good time."

He took them, while I walked around the car to the driver's seat. "John, I'm sorry, I —"

I got in the car and slammed shut the door. I started the car and roared off, leaving him standing there with my swimming trunks and a sad look on his face.

I couldn't dare. I just couldn't.

When I got home after driving around for a good two hours, I could hear my phone ringing as I unlocked the door. I threw open the door and lunged for the phone in the kitchen.

"Hello —" I said, breathless.

"Hey," said Scorpio. "You okay?"

"I just walked in."

"Mind if I come by?"

"I guess."

"Okay," he said, and hung up. He didn't sound happy. He arrived a few minutes later. I knew it took about half an hour to get to my sister's house from here, so where did he call from?

He knocked on my door and then opened it before I got to it. He was carrying his saddlebags from his bike. He looked down, a little embarrassed, I think. Then he looked up at me.

"I punched your brother in the face," he said, setting down the saddlebags near the door.

"What? Why?"

"He called you a fag in front of your mother."

I put my head in my hands.

"I know how you feel about that kind of shit," he continued, closing the door and walking over to me.

"What exactly did he say?"

"He said," with a really good approximation of my brother's voice, "'I think Johnny's a faggot.'"

"And you punched him in the face."

"In the pool. Julia had a fit and told me to leave."

The phone rang. I looked at it, wondering who was calling me. Was it my sister? Alex? My brother? I picked up the phone.

"Hello."

"John," said Julia, her voice cold, "Is that man there?"

"What man?"

"Scorpio."

"No, why?" I was looking right at him.

"Don't let him in your house, whatever you do. He's dangerous."

"Why?"

"He beat up Joey."

"What for?"

"Joey said something stupid. He was drunk. It was stupid."

"I'll be careful. Is Joey okay?"

"He broke his nose. Alex brought him to the hospital." She sighed. "I never should have let him in this house. He's very dangerous."

But I knew that. "Okay. Call me later about how Joey made out."

"Bye," she said, and hung up.

I put the phone back on its cradle, staring at Scorpio. He had his hands in his pockets and looked sufficiently chastened. I looked at the flowers on my kitchen table. *He means well*, I thought, not realizing that would be our mantra.

He asked, "What did she say I did?"

"You broke his nose."

"I meant to do that."

"She told me not to let you in my house. She said you were dangerous."

"I am dangerous, but to the right people."

"Not my brother, Scorpio. Please. I hadn't seen him in ages."

"Then he shouldn't have called you that."

I said quietly, "But it's true."

"You're not a faggot."

I winced when he used the word. That part was true: I didn't walk around acting like a typical light-in-the-loafers homosexual. But then, I couldn't. Not if I would be found out. That wasn't my natural tendency, anyway.

He came around the table and put his arms around me, drawing me into an embrace. I smelled the chlorine in his hair.

"I'll apologize. I'll pay for the damages. I'm sorry."

I rested against him, feeling his hard body, his heart beat through the t-shirt. "He went to the hospital."

"I'll have them send me the bill."

"Where?" I looked up at him. "Where are you going to be?"

He looked at me, his eyes soft, and kissed me, gentle and tender. "Right here with you."

A small voice inside me, a voice I had never heard before, said in my head, *Stop fighting it. Admit it to yourself and everyone.*

Admit what? I didn't want him to leave? That I actually felt proud when he had punched my brother in the face for calling me that dirty word? That maybe I did love him, too?

"What are you thinking?" he asked me.

"I don't know. A lot of things."

"About me?"

"Yeah, about you."

"About any certain part of me?"

I rubbed his back. "About all of you. What you're going to do to my life."

He chuckled. I lay my head on his chest, and he just held me, stroking my hair and neck.

There was a knock on the door.

I sighed. "Hell," I said, and disengaged from him. I walked over to the door and threw it open.

Joey stood on the other side with a bandage across his nose, Alex right behind him. "Hi," he said. "Is Scorpio in here?"

"I saw his bike outside," said Alex.

I stepped aside. Scorpio stepped forward so that he was in view from the door.

Alex appraised me, like I would get those looks in the bar, looks that meant *Should I take you home?* To see Alex looking at me that way was unnerving.

I turned away from Alex and shut the door. Joey sheepishly looked at Scorpio, then looked at me.

"I guess he told you what happened." He sounded pretty nasallly, due to the busted nose.

Scorpio crossed his arms.

"I'm sorry I called you a faggot, John."

"In front of mom," I said. "Of all people."

Joey said, "I don't think she believed me."

"She believed it. all right," said Alex. Alex glared at me. "She will when I tell her what went on in the shed between you two."

"What?" I blinked. "You were there, too!"

Joey looked from Alex to me, Alex's angry look and my shocked one. I had promised not to say anything.

"Alex," said Scorpio, his voice dropping an octave lower than usual, "Shut your fuckin' trap."

Alex whirled on Scorpio. "No. I've shut my trap for you long enough, you deviant."

"Lookit the pot calling the kettle black."

"Like anyone would believe you over me. I've been married sixteen years."

"To the first girl you knocked up by mistake." Scorpio pointed to his own chest. "What did you say in that shed? You wanted to suck my cock since the first minute you saw me. Like you did all those times in school. When I fucked you in the woods by the dorm. You fuckin' loved that shit. And now you're calling *me* a deviant?"

"I learned my lesson, Scorpio. *Arthur.*"

Scorpio smiled, but it was a cold smile, the one of someone who was ready to murder. "If you only knew, Alex."

"Okay, wait a second. Let's stop right here," I said, getting in between the two of them. That voice I mentioned took control, and I found myself saying, "Yes, I'm gay."

Joey smiled, and Alex looked disgusted. But it was a forced look, because his eyes watered up.

Alex took Joey's arm. "Let's get out of here."

Joey pulled his arm away. "He's my brother, man."

"Suit yourself. You'll both be on the outside looking in once I tell Julia what happened."

Scorpio moved faster than I thought a man could move. He reached beyond me and grabbed Alex by the hair, yanking him back. In his other hand was the switchblade he always carried, and he placed its tip at Alex's throat.

"You say one fuckin' word, and I'll fuck your daughter and make you fuckin' watch." He leaned closer. "And she'll fuckin' enjoy it, too. Like you did."

I gulped. "Scorpio, please. Let him go."

Scorpio scratched Alex's neck with the tip of the switchblade and threw him aside. He fell against the wall, rattling my pictures. Then Scorpio put the switchblade away and looked casually at Joey.

Alex touched his neck, his fingertips coming away with blood. Joey grabbed Ales by the arm and the two of them both bolted out of my apartment like they were escaping the clutches of a demon.

Scorpio sighed. "I'm sorry I had to do that."

He means well, I thought, as I hugged him.

www.ingramcontent.com/pod-product-compliance
Lightning Source LLC
Chambersburg PA
CBHW022106170626
46808CB00002B/630